Goof and Other Stories

Goof and Other Stories

Sean Enright

CREATIVE ARTS BOOK COMPANY
Berkeley • California

Goof and Other Stories is published by Donald S. Ellis
and distributed by Creative Arts Book Company

For information contact:
Creative Arts Book Company
833 Bancroft Way
Berkeley, California 94710
(800) 848-7789

ISBN 0-88739-314-4
Library of Congress Catalog Number 99-66709
Printed in the United States of America

To Ame

In memory:

William Patrick Lynch, Jr.
(1959-1995)
and
Suzanne Gerin
(1938-1996)

Acknowledgements

I'm grateful to my mother, two brothers, and four sisters, whose stories have been wholesaled here, many much livelier in their original tellings. Sister Sheila did a fine final copy-edit. Special thanks to brother Michael for his encouragment. Appreciation goes to Edward Parrot, Esq., for unwavering support and prickly insights. Steve Hayes was a crucial help in revising.

Table of Contents

Goof and Other Stories

Goof

The tiny things that crumbled in my stupid life over the past six months must have thrown a kink into the whole universe. It is the night before my birthday. I'll be fourteen. I just graduated from the eighth grade at St. Tabasco School, but it's really called St. John Bosco. St. John Bosco was a saint who liked children and had a lot of crazy dreams that the Pope told him to write down. When he was younger, he had been a juggler, and that way people gathered around him to watch him juggle and do tricks, and one of the tricks was that as soon as he got a crowd, he started preaching to them. One of his dreams was that he was watching all of these young guys fighting in a field, but then he became their leader and they all turned into sheep.

Next year I am going to high school with the Jesuits, who are supposedly going to want to kick my ass from here to Jupiter every single day. Like I'm so scared.

I am not getting along with anybody in my family. My father thinks I should play some sports and get a part-time job, even though I'm only in eighth grade. "Stop fooling around in that G.D. science lab," is his favorite thing to say. My ma is disappointed in me. Maud found out I necked with her best friend, who is a Polish girl named Margaret Grabaski, and Emmet is in trouble with his teacher, Mr. Man. My baby sister still likes me, but she likes everybody.

Necked is a funny way of describing what I did with Maud's friend. I think about my father necking when he was my age. He also spent a lot of time back then delivering papers on a bike for five cents a day, which is one of his favorite stories. Another one is that once he had a 107-degree fever for seven days, or maybe it was a 109-degree fever for seven days.

1

One number that is completely correct is that I pay 0 percent attention when he tells it because I've heard it so many times by now. He's the first one I ever heard say the word *necking*. It's like in my mind he becomes a swan, and his girl does too, and they are floating down a river rubbing their necks against each other.

From what I know about my father's mother whom we call Gram, she would have gone insane if she ever saw my father necking. She hates TV commercials and Protestants. I don't see her that often, but sometimes I go do her shopping for her. When my parents really need to go somewhere, sometimes she comes over and watches us. I think she probably would have knocked my father's lights out if she'd caught his goofy ass even trying to neck anywhere near her.

I know the feeling. You see, I'm a goof. I'm klutzy with stuff that's heavy or fragile. I act like a guy when I'm with guys and like a girl when I'm with girls. I sweat a lot over nothing. If I say the right thing it's at the wrong time. I'm tall enough to be considered big, overweight enough to be considered fat, and smart enough to be considered a sissy. I also have a good enough singing voice to be considered gay. I wear glasses, but they're cockeyed and slide down my nose because they've been broken so often. I use hair grease, but my hair still looks messy. My pants are usually too short and my ties don't tie right and I clean my ears annually and bite the skin around my fingers like it was cheese. You get the picture. Even my name is goofy. Digby Shaw. Shaw's not so bad, but nobody ever gets that far.

"Digby? Is that a word? Is that really your name?"

No, a-hole. I made it up so no one would ever know who I was.

Maybe if I describe myself, you can imagine what I look like, but it could be impossible. In the first place, I'm pale, so it's easy to look past me. My features just hang in the white space where my skin is. You know the Cheshire Cat? I'm the Cheshire Cat with love handles.

I don't act like I'm fat. Usually if you're fat, you act fat. You jiggle and have a squeaky voice and you won't make eye contact because you're used to people not looking you in the eyes, because you're fat. Not me. I keep my arms straight down my sides, and my love handles don't jiggle, and my voice is in the middle, or at least the upper middle. I always hurry to make eye contact, because whoever makes eye contact first wins.

My eyes are grayish. That is BY FAR the blandest of all colors. My eyes are slitty, which is the most common kind of eye. They're a little tired-looking, but that's from too much sleep, not too little. My eyelashes are long, or at least that's what Maxine Myna once told me when we were having a fake-hitting, pre-make-out session that never did make it to the real making-out session (unfortunately).

Maxine said she wished she had eyelashes like mine. This is not the sexiest thing a girl has ever said to a guy, so then I was nervous it would get around that I had these fluffy curly eyelid hairs (which is all they really are, even though people dress them up and call them lashes).

I guess I don't have to worry about her blabbing because it would make her look just as bad to admit that she got that close to me as it made ME look for having nice eyelashes. If she even told anyone, which I seriously doubt she did. I'm not the kind of person who gets told about. I'm the person who listens to other people telling stuff about other people, if you know what I mean. (If you don't know what I mean, you can stick around anyway.)

My mouth looks wet all the time, like a piece of red felt. I have at least one zit at all times. My ears look like Mr. Potato Heads, my nails are skanky, and I chafe in the summer and get a lot of crotch rot (I chafe in the winter too, but it doesn't get as red). That's some of what I look like.

I just graduated from eighth grade, and in three months I have to go start my whole life over again in high school where I'm sure I'll be abused by everyone in sight. (You're darn tooting I'm scared.)

Anyway, if I can get it all down, somehow, truthfully, starting with me, and just try to remember the whole truth about what happened in the past year, it might be worth it. It was just the second half of eighth grade. It was no big whup. But for some reason it felt unusual to me, like it was a time that would never happen again. I think I committed a million venial sins, as usual, but was totally innocent of mortal sin right through ('til the end, anyway). It doesn't matter what the count was, really, of my sins or my penance. I seriously doubt that there is a big score book up in heaven. But there is a big book right here in front of me, on my desk. It's my scrapbook. It's where I keep crazy old stuff that I saved because I was too much of a dumb-ass to just throw the stuff away when I first got it.

Everybody always says that the best place to start is the beginning, but as usual that's because they're telling you to do something that they don't have to do. The beginning is also the hardest place to start, because it's way back there. The easiest place to start would be the end, which is where I am now, sitting at the desk in my bedroom, looking out the window, watching Emmet trying to walk on grass in the backyard with-out leaving any trace, which is something he picked up from some damn book on Geronimo.

There were two things that I started, though. I did an experiment where a sea urchin's eggs got fertilized without a male; and I fell in, and out, of love with Maxine Myna like she was some kind of revolving door. They were two important things, though. They showed me something about how it was going to be to be me, living my life.

My sea urchin, Strongy, ended up dying, but nobody even noticed except for me, and even I had to look twice, because she didn't look a lot different dead than she did alive. I don't think she felt any pain at all. My advisor for the science fair, this woman named Dr. Bonham, said pain in lower animals is something scientists don't understand.

She was the mother of this tall guy in my class. Actually, she was a dermatologist, but she was cool and she never reminded me that I had acne, which my ma is constantly reporting to me. "Oh, you have a bump!" my ma says. She doesn't mean for it to be mean. But I know when I have a zit. I know before anybody. I don't think my ma has ever had a single zit, but I would have to check on that.

Did that sound like a Stridex commercial or what?

I got to know this dermatologist, Dr. Bonham, during my enzymes project last year. I went over to the Bonham's house after school one day, and she gave me her old medical school textbooks. They had cool grue-some pictures of burn victims in them who the doctors were trying to heal with enzymes. The books had that old sleazy smell, and a couple had some pretty horny pictures in them.

You might think I'm a pervert because I say that, but you always have to think about the bright side of everything that happens to you or you'll go crazy, like Danny Dens did. The way I see it, the horny-looking pic-tures of patients could be pretty depressing, if you just thought about them being sick. But they're not just sick, they're also naked as jaybirds. So that's something. And the spooky thing is that all the patients had their eyes covered with long, thin pieces of black tape. Their goosebumps looked white, with some gray in it.

Burn victims really didn't have much to do with my project. I was busy filling test-tubes with spit and hydrochloric acid and then putting different kinds of food in the tubes to see how fast they would be digest-ed. Bread gets soggy, and meat goes all pulpy, and they both end up dissolving completely, so I had to time it right so they could still be recognizable on judging day, but real eaten-into at the same time. I got 3rd Place and Honorable Mention at the County Science Fair.

But I figured I'd take whatever Dr. Bonham had. After all, she was a doctor, and it helps to know all kinds of weird stuff, in case you have to talk your way past the judges because your results were inconclusive. It would be nice to be honest about scientific results, but it doesn't always work that way.

Strongy was a green sea urchin (*Strongylocentrototus drobachiensis*) from the Gulf of Maine. Most people think sea urchins are plants when they first see them, but they're not. They're animals, but very primitive. Strongy loved cold water, 12 degrees Celsius or even lower. I collected eggs from her in February. She was cruising along great under laboratory conditions, but she got fairly famous near the end of this story, in the spring time. The traveling to and from the school and County Science Fair finally caught up with her. Now it's almost June.

It took me four days to discover she was dead. One thing about sea urchins is they look pretty much the same dead or alive. I was moving her from the table in my laboratory to the utility shelf, and she flipped over onto her back. Usually she stayed clamped to the side on the glass, but she was dead. It made me sad, but what are you going to do? When I say laboratory, I mean the corner of our laundry room. It's really just an old aluminum table with my chemistry set on it. I kept Strongy's water cold, and she ate like a pig, mostly food like algae and scum. Sea urchins eat using this thing called Aristotle's lantern, which is made up of five hard plates that come together like a beak that they use to scrape the algae right off of rocks.

Strongy's mouth was located on the underside of her body, and she took dumps through her a-hole, which was on top, so she was something you had to know a few things about, if you were going to go to kiss her. Sea urchins like the dark, so I kept Strongy's tank covered with an old gray coat of my father's that was lying around in the laundry room.

There's an old burglar alarm I made hanging by its guts from the pegboard above the laundry room door. I made it out of an old hair dryer of my sister Maud's. It only worked once and then the motor burned out, but I still tell my little brother Emmet it works so he'll stay away from my stuff. He's a nimrod, and believes just about any of the strange crap I tell him.

I have all these *Popular Mechanics* in bundles tied with strings, and one of them had instructions on building an airplane in your garage, but I didn't have squat of the parts that you needed, so that was that. Usually I just flipped through them and looked at the machines and engines and hoped that there would be bomb recipes. But there was always way too much information.

Anyway, I canned Strongy behind the shed in the backyard in a Hellman's Mayonnaise jar. Then I dug her up three months later to show Emmet what she looked like, because he thought she might have completely disappeared. The salt water left in the jar had turned gray.

We could still see her spines pressed flat against the glass, like a little wet broom. When a sea urchin dies, all its spines fall off, leaving this shell they call the test. If you look carefully at Strongy's test, you can see the little bumps covering it where her spines once connected. Strongy was cool. She could rotate each one of her spines inside those bumps.

I share a bedroom with Emmet, which sucks. I made him put his bed so it faces the wall. The rule is that he has to knock first on the wood of the furniture if he wants to talk to me. It's just your basic boring bedroom. I have a desk, which I like a lot. It has this board you pull out to write on, and there are two bumper stickers on the board. The first bumper sticker is a Pippy Longstocking one, which was pretty gay of me, but I was just a little kid when I put it on there, and now it won't come off. She's the little girl who's so strong and lives in a house alone with her horse and has two little brother-and-sister friends. The other bumper sticker is a Right To Life March one, which we got for free last year in school.

There's a poster of Frank Howard stuck on the back of the bedroom door. He was a huge Washington Senators outfielder, but they became the Texas Rangers, so now he could go to hell, even though he was almost seven feet tall. He wore glasses, but he was still an excellent player, and the poster was life-size, so it just about covered the entire door.

I've carved my initials all over the place on the desk, and I've carved the initials of some girls in there, too. Then when I started hating them I tried to carve out their initials back into my initials, which didn't always work, so the wood basically looks like some munched-out termites got at it.

In the lab, there's a lot of chemical glassware that me and my best friend Peter Kiernan scrounged up from the dumpsters up behind the medical school, before he moved away to Michigan to go to a School Without Walls. Some of the beakers that we got looked pretty scary. We had no clue what was in them. But Peter said that if we boiled the hell out of them that would make them 100 percent safe, and since I haven't gotten leukemia yet, I guess he was right.

The ceiling isn't finished in the laundry room where my lab is, so there's all of this insulation sticking out from the rafters. I have some stuff hidden up there, including an unopened can of Schlitz Malt Liquor (the one that has the bull on it) that I found up by the highway. (I'm not going to drink it. Beer sucks. It tastes like something's wrong with it. I figured I'd hang onto the can, just in case I ever needed it.)

I also hid these dirty words up in the rafters. They go to the song "Both Sides Now," and I will get killed for it if my ma ever discovers I wrote them. (I don't worry much about my father finding it—he almost never goes downstairs.) This was in sixth grade, in case you think I'm still gross and immature. I just took the words to the song, like...

> *I've looked at life from both sides now-*
> *from in and out, and upside down...*

and I flipped them around and made them dirty. In my lyrics, this girl is singing about what happens inside her body. It's stupid. I'm holding on to it because it's so dirty that I don't know how to get rid of it. (That's sort of cool, how scary that is.) I know other dirty stuff, of course, but it's memorized in my head so only I know I know it:

> *I received an invitation*
> *From the Board of Education*
> *To conduct an operation on a girl*
> *I stuck my dickalation*
> *In her lower ventilation*
> *To increase the population of the world.*

I feel guilty that I have the song hidden away in the ceiling, but guilt is a weird thing. I'm just starting to get into it. I have to think about it from time to time because at school we have to go to Confession once a month.

Confession is scary. You go in a dark little booth and kneel down. There's one tiny stained-glass window in there that lets in a tiny little sheet of purple-and-blue light that you can wiggle your fingers in the middle of. You wait in there and you run through your list, which is always this:

> *Bless me father for I have sinned, it's been*
> *about a month since my last confession and these*
> *are my sins: I was mean to my brother and*
> *sisters 5-to-10 times, I talked back to my*
> *parents 7-to-12 times, and I cussed 5 times.*

Like I said before, the numbers don't matter. The priest isn't listening for your numbers. He's only listening for the last thing you say, because he has a whole line of kids who are coming in right after you, and the last thing you say is all he can remember, so he asks you two or three questions about it to make sure you're not B.S.-ing, and then he gives you a short speech. So you can't lie about the last sin, because you're going to have to talk about it a little, but you can usually lie about the other ones. The trick is not to take too long. Short lies only.

When it's over, you feel great. You feel like you're in a sneaker commercial and it's time to jump up and touch the moon. But I never know if I feel great because I've confessed my sins, or because I don't have to go back for a whole nother month. (Probably both.)

Some things feel like they are wrong when you're doing them but aren't wrong, like sticking up for yourself in front of a crowd who doesn't care about you, and you get embarrassed and feel a little sick to your stomach. Some things feel great, but people say that they're wrong (like you know exactly what). The good thing is that you just confess what you can, which is never very much. You could never confess everything—it would take too long. It would take infinity.

> Here's another dirty song from out of my brain:
> *Beat your meat on the toilet seat*
> *Doo dah, doo dah*
> *Hands get tired use your feet*
> *Oh the doo dah day*

❀ ❀ ❀

The President resigned last year at the end of the summer, and that was fine by me. I hated Nixon, but then I got sick of Watergate too, because it was too complicated in the newspaper. I'd have to stop all the time when I was reading and try to remember who was who. My friend Slim Mars's (his real name is Solomon) mother knew a lot about it, but besides her and my father, I didn't know anybody who didn't think it was boring and that the hearings kept a lot of good stuff off TV. Ford is the president now, but my father says he sneaked in. He pardoned Nixon on September 8 last year, which was the first week of school. He probably shouldn't have. He's not doing the greatest job, but my dad says he's okay compared to Nixon, even though the eight percent unemployment rate is higher than it's been since 1941, when my dad had his job for five cents a day.

Emmet thought Watergate was an amusement park ride. He kept bugging my ma about it once when she was trying to write checks for the bills, and we were supposed to be getting ready for bed. My father was reading a book. I've only seen him read the newspaper a couple of times, on Sundays. Emmet wanted to know what a water-gate was, and whether you got splashed when you rode down through it. Then Molly started wetting herself because she had heard the word splash. Before you know it, they were both in bathing suits by the door, waiting to drive to the park, instead of being in their pajamas brushing their teeth, and my ma had to calm them down, and explain to them about reality.

My father did tell me some good graffiti about Nixon once, when my ma wasn't listening in. It goes like this: you write in big bold letters DICK NIXON BEFORE HE DICKS YOU. There's also something you can type on a typewriter, but it takes a long time.

```
 !      !     !       !        !       (   )   !       !

 !!     !     !       !        !       (   )   !!      !

 ! !    !     !              !          (   )   !  !   !

 !   ! !     !       !        !       (   )   !      ! !

 !      !     !       !        !       (___)   !       !
```

My father can type it as fast as a bullet with only two fingers. Hunt and peck, he calls it. He said when Nixon resigned he was going to win

150 dollars that he'd bet someone at work, but later he said the guy had beat him on a technicality, because the bet was that Nixon would be gone within a year of the break-in, but it took longer. (I have made two bets in my whole life, both on the Ali-Frazier fights, and I lost both of them.)

At least when Nixon resigned there weren't any more riots. I would hate to be caught in a riot. I would go down like a sack of crap. I kid you not—I am that slow. I worried that the high school I wanted to go to downtown was going to become a crime zone if there were riots. They still haven't cleaned up from the riots they had there seven years ago.

My father used to say that I would probably get drafted to go to Vietnam. He was very pessimistic about Vietnam. Nobody seemed to want to talk about it too much anymore, except that it was too bad. Now it seems to go on and on, on its own. Nobody says we lost except my father. He says it all the time.

My Lame Scrapbook

Catholics like to talk about how we get persecuted by other religions, and about how that's because Catholics are the real true religion. But I think anybody can be a creep if he wants to. It doesn't matter what religion you are. It's true, though, that people who aren't Catholics don't know much about them. People think Catholics are always either:

1) saving lives;
2) not eating meat;
3) praying; or
4) doing something with their fifteen children.

But we're not. We're more normal than that, anyway. Usually we're just like everybody else. We're either:

1) feeling bad;
2) waiting to use the phone;
3) wishing;
4) not saying something; or
5) trying to remember something.

Every day I remember more of the stuff I had imagined the day before. With all that proof of being awake, my old daydream almost never strikes. It was awesome, because in it I had fallen asleep in the third grade, and soon I was going to wake up, and everything that had piled up since I fell asleep that one night five years ago was going to be wiped out.

Back then there were real saints and they scared you. God was a cloud you sat on, where you closed your eyes and asked for stuff and complained. Jesus saw every thought you had like your brain was typing it out and handing it around. Each Christmas morning was always like the day you were born all over again, except you enjoyed it more now that you weren't a pathetic baby with no muscle.

Sometimes I wish that instead of being born the usual way, I had been flown through the solar system to earth and just dropped off here. It would be much simpler than having to have been nothing first. But I wasn't flown in. I was born, so I have to deal with it.

I remember the third grade because that was the year I started my lame scrapbook with a bunch of stuff in it that's been folded for too long, so it's all starting to tear. At first I just saved stuff, because it seemed to be too hard to remember everything. Then all of a sudden, halfway through this year, it seemed like I couldn't forget anything. I'd lie awake at night, waiting for car lights to light up the wall across from my bed, when they come scrambling in through the blinds. A lot of this story is what I have been remembering. But something like my friend Peter Kiernan moving away doesn't fit into a scrapbook. I don't even have a picture of him.

Two years before he moved away, Peter had proved once and for all that he was brave by showing Jake Myna that he wasn't afraid of him. We were in the sixth grade, and Peter and I had gone to the library to look up stuff in the encyclopedia. We looked up the word "Sex" (five entries), "Titty" (no entry, but there was a little illustration of Lake Titicaca on the same page, which we did check out), the word "Butt" (zero entries), and then we looked up the entry "McGovern" because that was what my oral report was going to be on. There were two entries.

Jake came around the corner. His whole seventh-grade class was having their library period. You'll hear more about Jake Myna later on. He used to be my best friend. Now I don't know. It's complicated, because I was in love with his sister.

We were having social studies but were being let out to go to the library in twos to look through the encyclopedia. Our sixth-grade teacher's name was Mrs. Blurt, and she was the oldest teacher in the whole school who wasn't a nun. She was seventy-two years old, and her teeth were the same color as her skin. She wore red lipstick that didn't fill in the little lines in her lips all the way. There were gaps.

Jake hissed at me.

"Shaw! C'mere! I want you to see something."

Peter and I walked over to between the Science & Technology shelves where Jake was standing. He had a can of Lysol in one hand and book of matches in the other. I knew what he was going to do. He was going to make a flame-thrower. We'd done the same thing a bunch of times in the lab at home, so it was no big whup. Spray paint worked better, because it was heavier, and the flame got thrown farther.

Still, I was a little bit interested. It might be a good showoff in front of Peter, if we could go out in the woods behind the parish groundskeeper's house, who supposedly shot rocksalt at kids who trespassed on his property.

"Where'd you get that huge can of Lysol?" I asked Jake.

"From Way Gross' stuff in the bucket-room." Way Gross was the janitor. "C'mon, let's light it. We can do it between the magazine stacks behind Mrs. Rule's desk."

Mrs. Rule was the librarian, and I was 100 percent not interested in bothering her. Besides being a pussy, a coward, and worried that getting caught making a flame-thrower would make my grades go down, I also really liked Mrs. Rule. She had been the librarian since I was in the first grade. She liked me because I liked to read books. I liked her because she liked me.

"You're crazy, Jake. No way. Save it and we'll do it on the way home, under the bridge. I got some Black Cats, too." Those were firecrackers.

"C'mon, don't be a wimp." Jake looked at Peter. "Can't you leave your boyfriend behind for a minute or two?"

I looked at Peter, and smiled like Jake was only joking. Jake has a way of joking that isn't funny, though. When Jake does something funny, somebody's going to cry, even if everybody else laughs. Peter just looked back at me. And then he looked straight at Jake and said, "Simmer down, Jake."

"What was that, sweetie?"

"Don't get mad, Jake. You can still light matches without Digby, can't you?"

"Well, you're smart and pretty, aren't you? I'll bet you wouldn't do anything bad in a million years, would you? You would feel so *bad*. You might even cry."

Peter turned back to me. "I'm gonna cruise back to Blurto's, Digby. I'll see you there."

"Okay, Peter. I'll be there in a minute."

Peter started to walk away. Jake watched him and then called after him, "Bye-bye for now, Pattycakes!"

"Whatsa matter, Jake, didn't you get enough hugs when you were a baby?" Peter didn't even turn around as he said it, but then Jake caught up with him and popped him in the mouth with the side of the Lysol can, and Peter got a fat lip. He still didn't tell on him, and Jake never bothered him again. We didn't make the flame-thrower, then. There was blood and Way Gross had to come with his mop. Peter said he tripped because the floor was slippery, and Way Gross looked at Mrs. Rule and his tooth glimmered like he was saying, "Not my fault I wax the floors so good."

The first thing in the scrapbook is from Creative Carousel, September 1962. It's a washed-out blue ribbon with the edges beginning to fray a little bit, like the fringe on a pair of cut-off jeans. It says, *First Place, Vertical Box Climb*. (I don't remember it at all, but my ma says it's true, it was called Infant Field Day, and that every baby won something.) So that's something.

The next thing is a few pages of my grade school yearbook from the first grade, June 1967. There is a black-and-white shot of the old church, when the priest used to keep his back to the congregation, and a long line of girls wearing veils going down the aisle for Holy Communion. Then there's a photo of Monsignor Bronk in cat glasses sitting with the Home-School Committee, all women. Three out of four of them have cat glasses, too. Actually, Monsignor's glasses are just real dorky, black and pointy, and not really cat glasses at all.

Molly still has cat glasses. It's almost like a disease. You think they've gone away completely, cat-glasses, but they're just hiding among small children.

In the scrapbook, the third thing is from 1969. It's a Polliwog Club membership card from the Young Men's Christian Association swimming pool, signed by the chairman of the Aquatic Committee. On the back of it there's a list of what I had to do to make Polliwog. Number 2 is Adjustment To Water, and #12 is Bobbing With Rhythmic Breathing.

There's a polliwog design on top of the YMCA emblem on the front of the card in the upper left corner. The toes look like they're already webbed, so technically it's really not a polliwog anymore.

I have discovered something else interesting in there, too, something besides every birthday card I have ever gotten since I was four. It's a copy of the newspaper from April 4, 1974. The headline says.

Hank Aaron Passes Babe Ruth.

He was forty years old, which is amazing. He just hung around and hung around and kept chipping away until he did it. He beat the Babe. It was the Braves at Cincinnati, his first cut, in the first inning of the first game of the season. The Braves lost, but who cares?

The guy who caught the ball had to give it back. All winter long the news on TV and in the paper was about how Hammerin' Hank was gonna do it, but then he did it the first day of the season. (Everybody knew it was going to be some time in the first week or so.) Then the news guys all shut up right away and acted like it wasn't a big thing anymore that had happened, now that it had gone ahead and happened, which shows you how fake the whole thing was.

There's a Black Velvet whiskey ad in the same newspaper, on the second page of the sports section. A MAN LIKES TO COME HOME TO BLACK VELVET. In it there's this skinny babe wearing a wet-looking black dress with big white buttons. She's lying on her side in mid-air looking up at the words A MAN like they're about to swoop down and start tickling her. When Gram comes over, my ma drinks a Rob Roy, which is made with whiskey, but not Black Velvet Whiskey. Rob Roy was this Scottish guy who fought against his own king, which shows you how bright he was. Maybe he was drunk.

Get used to it. I like to read long, boring, detailed stuff out loud. You never know what you might need to know. I always volunteer to read everything in class, any time, since I have learned I'm going to get called on anyway. I got glasses in the fifth grade and (as I mentioned) I'm big for my age. Husky, my ma says. Fat, as my father has been know to add. Glasses and fat make you a target. The teachers target you, if no one else in the class is answering. They look out over all of the little sleepy heads, and they see your glasses shining in mid-air, like all your bright ideas were made out of metal, and then they call on you.

They do it even if you usually volunteer a lot, but maybe you're taking a break right at that moment, because you don't know or you're tired. The teachers think all you do is sit inside and read because you're too fat to play sports. That's partly true, but not fair.

I can memorize pretty good, too. In the 4th and 5th grades I got to play Jesus two years in a row, in the Passion Play at Easter. Then Monsignor Bronk found out and went ape-shit. It was right after I brought a triangle into the confessional with me and clanged it before he was done on the other side. He came right out of his area and right through the curtain into my booth where I was and yelled at me for being sacrilegious, but Jake Myna had bet me three bucks I wouldn't do it.

Monsignor Bronk told Sister Ted right in front of the whole class that I didn't need a career being a savior, and so I had to play Barrabas, which is some reward. I mean, it wasn't like I was trying to walk on water or anything. Slim Mars played a Roman soldier and he got to chant, "We want Barrabas, we want Barrabas." Sometimes he still shouts it at me when I'm off-guard and then he runs a couple feet away so I can't reach him. Slim can be a complete mongoloid some times.

Now I'm reading from last Sunday's bulletin. This is the Communion meditation in it:

> —You are the salt of the earth... You are
> the light of the world. (Mt. 5:13-14) To
> be effective in the world today, I must use
> a method of witnessing called infiltration.
> How can I infiltrate my society as a son and
> servant of the living God?

What was I reading a minute ago? Yeah, the newspaper ads. So flare pants are okay, but bell bottoms are a little gay. I was afraid to wear flares for a while. My father always wears straight legs (but most of the time they're a little bit floody, so you can see his socks crumbling down around his ankles).

I have started wearing a blue velour shirt that makes me look like I think I look muscular. I rub the velour in one direction and it doesn't look so shiny. Darwin Mars wears bell bottom pants that make his butt look like a girl's, really round and with a definite crack, but he's a hippie and a general waste of space.

Now I have all these new memories from the past six months to put in the scrapbook.

My neighborhood is not really a crazy place. It's a pretty normal place. It's even boring in a lot of ways. There are about four kinds of houses and 100 examples of each kind. They're painted different, but that's it—it's the same frigging house, usually, if you just look twice.

But you can't just look twice. You look three times, and four times, and so on, and then there's two ways to go: you can keep looking and always see the same old thing, or you can start dreaming up stuff. I like to dream up stuff. It's less boring that way than to keep living in the same dumb house with the same stupid family in the same old state.

I think Peter was pretty glad to leave. I mean, I think he still misses me—he's not a total dick—but he's happier out there in Michigan because it's an adventure. I don't blame him. He just moved away two weeks ago. Peter Kiernan was a nerdy brain with a bent dick. I've seen it, but we're not moes. It's bent near the top, and that's disgusting, but life goes on. Peter wouldn't even kill me for telling you about it. He has never spazzed out once in his life.

For a while, back in the fifth grade, he would weigh his books when he got home to measure how much homework he was getting. Then he started writing letters to the archbishop, and he enclosed graphs of increases in homework poundage, and his Aunt Floss followed up with a letter threatening our parish with a lawsuit. (Peter got a doctor to write up a report that he had injured his shoulders and his arms by carrying so many books home.)

His parents were hard to figure out because they didn't seem to be hard to figure out. They were just like him, only they acted even younger. They would do anything Peter told them to do if he had only told them to do it, but he always behaved perfectly and wouldn't think of telling them to do anything. They loved him, like he was their oldest brother in a family where an oldest brother is actually loved. (Unlike my family, where the oldest brother is hated by kids and adults alike. Even Gram sneers at me a lot.)

I got a letter from Peter yesterday. He was going to be in a speech contest at a junior college, for God's sake. He was always advanced. In the letter he quoted part of the speech he was doing. It was something Martin Luther King had written:

> Hence, the forging of grand qualities of character is taking place daily and monthly as the struggle for a goal of a high moral end is pursued. What will this mean to the future? There will come from this cauldron a mature man experienced in life's lessons...

At the bottom of it, it said, "Don't read the underlined parts of this letter to your family." (There was red underlining all the cusses.) Another part of the letter said:

> I have to ride a goddamn bus to school which is not like walking. Do me a favor - go by our old house and see if there's a pair of cleats in the window-well, and if there is, mail them to me.

> P.S. Don't you hate P.S.es?

> P.P.S You'll probably see our car there- my father is still trying to sell it.

I went by his house. Sure enough their old car was still there, so I got in it. (It was locked, but one window was cracked.) I sat in it for a while and got completely sad. I had a can of shaving cream with me just in case, so I thought I'd put some on all the windows so nobody would want to buy it, and maybe Peter's family would have to come back home to pick it up and take it back to Michigan to try to sell it. While I was doing this a guy came up in a car and I was busted.

"What the fuck is this?" he yelled as he got out. He looked about as old as my father. I felt mostly stupid but a little scared, too. "Wipe that crap off now and get out." So I wiped it off. When he was leaving I saw him pull a metal sign out of the trunk of his car and stick it in their grass. I should have brought Ricky Seerser along with me and sicked him on the dude.

The back of our yard is up against the fence between our house and the Seerser's house. They have this kid, Ricky, who's mentally retarded. Ricky's almost never allowed out at night, but once in a while he'll come out in his pajamas and stand underneath his dunk-court basket and roll in a few buckets. When it's warm out and the windows are open, he gurgles as his mother gets him ready to go to bed. Behind the screen he talks out loud out to the dark.

"All finished now? All go home now?"

Ricky always says the same six or seven words because that's all he knows. He never speaks in sentences and he almost always says, "Wet pants!" at the end of whatever he says. When we're out playing or doing something else in the street, like getting a ball that went down the sewer, he'll sit on his bike watching us with his feet pressed flat against the asphalt. His mom comes to collect him and bring him back to their house for dinner.

She says, "Say good-bye to your friends, Ricky." But we're not really his friends, he just watches us. He doesn't even know *how* to play, really.

"Hello," Ricky says. Then he turns and follows his mom down the street, just pushing off with his feet and coasting behind her, then pushing off with his feet again. At least he can ride a bike. When Ricky is riding, he pedals slowly with his knees going way out in front of him, almost farther out than the tires. His elbows stick out to the side like wings.

Ricky was too big for the kid's bike he rode, but he was a squeeb so he didn't know that. He just knew he loved his bike. His mother once tried to take it away from him and replace it with a brand-new ten-speed, but Ricky howled and walked up and down the street and tossed the same brick through five car windows. He smashed the glass in each window, then reached in and pulled the brick out and walked to the next car and did the same thing. There were bloody scratches on his bicep. Then we heard Mrs. Seerser run down the front steps screaming. She threw up the garage door and wheeled out his old gay bike.

Peter Kiernan's gone now, but at least I still have a squeeb living behind me. I can always go shoot hoops with him, I guess. At least I'd win.

Torture

D arwin Mars was the evil older brother of my small friend Solomon Mars. Darwin has multiple zit welts on his neck and long hair like Charles Manson. He has given me all of my science project ideas since I was in the fourth grade, and they were all winners.

Unfortunately, since he started going to high school downtown (he's three years older than me), he's begun hanging out with low-life types and maggot potheads. I had been hoping he would start to sleep in a little more often, since lately he was everywhere I went and I couldn't take the punishment much longer.

When I say that my friend Slim Mars was my small friend, I mean it, but I should say a little bit more about that, because it makes me sound mean. Really what's happening is that I just keep getting older, and people are getting meaner. Even though I try to stay the same, I think I am getting meaner, too. Also, I'm more *his* friend than he is *my* friend, if you have ever had that feeling. (Deep down I have a sneaky feeling that Slim may be more of a goof than me.)

But he lived right on the street behind our street, so it was hard to avoid him. Also, he had a hoop in his backyard, and his mother stocked Fudgetowns, which were things for the Plus column. At school, if someone else was talking, or if I was just walking along with someone else, and Slim showed up, sometimes I ignored him. He didn't seem to mind, which was why we were still slightly friends.

On June 14, 1963 (I'm reading out loud), patent application # 3235259 for "Toy Boxers" was filed by Marvin I. Glass, Harry Disko, and Burton G. Meyer. In the toy stores it was called Rockem Sockem Robots. The black-and-white patent sketch has two figures: figure 1 is a corner view from above, with the boxers in "en garde" position touching gloves; and figure 2 is from the same angle, with the lefthand boxer in mid-power-hand. The righthand boxer has been caught flatfooted. He has one solid head ("block") and one drawn with dotted lines "knocked off" an inch above the solid one.

If I try to picture how Darwin Mars beat *me* up one day back in January, I will need to think of a Rockem Sockem ring with three boxers. That's right—three. Darwin and Rafe Biktor would be the regular boxers, like I described above, but the third would be a not-scary-looking, very weird shape, smack in the center of the ring, which would be me, looking like a five-year-old with a case of elephantitis that allowed him to pass as an eighth-grader. I had a knee on my chest, my eyes were being jammed by several fingers at one time, and I got that queer cast-iron taste in my mouth, which I always taste right after I get smacked on my nose.

Getting beaten up was sort of Rockem Sockem robots, but much worse, really. Darwin and Rafe were on me in a step. The bus driver floored it, ignoring my pitiful waving at him. Darwin (I guess since he was the one who knew me) got to hit me first. He flamed up karate-style, his big Nazi hippie boots coming straight at me like the ones in the "Keep On Truckin'" bumper sticker. Then he spun around and rabbit-punched me in the throat. I was too stunned by his windmilling to react. My respiration was cut and I blacked out.

Next thing I remembered after Darwin hit me, I was crouched down choking on bus fumes. I didn't even have the strength to pick the gravel out of my wrist. At one point, I did try to stand up, only to receive a crushing back-flip from Rafe. He had been standing behind Darwin the whole time, smiling like it was not going to be a real mugging but actually planning how to serve me up my next sucking chest wound. (I really did try to stand up. I'm cowardly but big.)

Rafe resembled a weasel with the weasel's pointy ears and the real short brush-cut hair, and a huge khaki-colored birthmark under one of his ears. His sister, who was in my grade, was the definition of turd. She acted like she was prissy, but I have also heard her cuss, and cuss pretty good, so you make the call. Plus she was completely flat, if not even a little bit caved-in.

❀ ❀ ❀

Before I make myself look like a martyr just because I got beat up by two high school guys, being physically mauled was not something really new to me. Wedgies (bevs and nelsons), swats, pinkbellies, Chinese rope burns, tittie twisters (my sister Maud calls them purple hermies), charlie horses, dick-fights, skull thwacks, Spocks, lock-loogies—I had them all.

For a Chinese rope burn you really need two torturers, one to hold the victim's arm really tight so he can't move, and the other to grab the forearm with both hands and then turn his hands in opposite directions. This twists the arm-flesh and burns the little hairs. It kills. For a charlie horse, you just come at the person from the side, and ask, "Who won at the racetrack today?" and then you knee the person hard in the middle of his thigh, and yell, "Charlie horse!"

Skull thwacks are when you flick your middle finger against somebody's skull or ear really hard like you're flicking a marble. For Spocks, you grab a guy by the shoulder like on *Star Trek* and pinch down and try to make him pass out. It hurts like hell, but you don't have to pass out, just give out at the knees a little and sag down, and usually the person will let go. Lock-loogies I've only heard about, because you need to have a locker, so you have to be in high school, but the deal is that you hack up a really serious hunk of lung-cheese, then you flip over a person's lock and dangle a loogie right down onto the metal. When the person comes up and grabs his lock to open it, his hand will get covered with snot. That's not really physically torture, but it's so gross it almost is.

Of course, in the eighth grade we weren't really supposed to be doing this stuff anymore. Most everybody seemed more interested in other things. But once in a while, a bunch of guys would form a pack and go waste somebody.

I have received wedgies when my underpants are clean, and wedgies when my underpants are dirty. A bev is a wedgie when your underpants are grabbed from the back, a nelson is from the front, and a half-nelson is from the side but doesn't really work very well. I've been testing it out on my little brother, Emmet. In a wedgie, your dees get pulled straight up out of your pants, so the little underneath bridge-part digs into your crack, and your nads get cramped together, like jellybeans. In a nelson the same things happen, but in reverse order. If you're a little guy and you get a bev, you can be hung from a hook in a locker. Again, you need a locker here, so you have to wait until high school, unless you go to public school, where they sometimes have lockers in elementary.

You get swats after you get a haircut. All the guys in your class line up and slap you across the back of the neck, where the hair was cut the shortest. It stings, but not for very long. Most guys try to get their hair cut on Fridays. I used to try to stay home sick the first couple of days after I got my haircut, but people usually noticed anyway. The hair doesn't have much time to grow back.

We used to have dickfights in sixth grade. It was in the boy's bathroom. If you're right-handed (like me) you cover your crotch up with your left hand and crouch over and slouch around in a circle around your opponent, and you keep your right hand cupped out in front of you. Then you try to rack the other dude's balls before he racks yours.

As I was kneeling there, I remembered the dream again, my daydream that I had fallen asleep in the third grade. This was the time I usually thought about it, just when something bad was happening to me that I wanted to stop. But I didn't want to just stop time, I wanted to reverse it and work back through all the stuff before the bad thing. I'd go straight back until I reached third grade again, writing capital letters in cursive on the board and falling in love with this substitute teacher we had, Mrs. Sharon Beau, who threw out the regular class lesson plan and talked about science all day long. She had a Southern accent and just loved kids. My weird friend George Gack liked her too, because she used Oil of Olay on her skin and she would let him smell her wrist. At first she had been a nurse, which was why she liked science so much.

If I saw Mrs. Beau at the store, she'd ask me how I was, and then talk to my ma.

"He's a joy in the classroom, Mrs. Shaw. He has real promise."

"Well, we're trying to get him to settle down, Mrs. Beau. But I'm afraid he's always trying to be a jack-of-all-trades."

But then I always hear this bursting noise, which is the daydream losing steam. Suddenly I'm back where I started, which this time was on my knees in the gravel, peering up at Darwin and Rafe. They both hooted and laughed. Darwin tossed a crumpled-up piece of paper at my face, and the both of them took off down the street for home, with their hands in their back pockets. Darwin lit a cig. A gust of smoke came over his shoulder like a scarf.

I got up really slow and uncrumpled the paper. It was a page from a biology book: Parthenogenesis, it said. It's artificial reproduction. Bees do it naturally, but I used sea urchins. It's complicated so I'll explain later. I started reading the page Darwin threw at me as I walked. And who turned up the path after I took my first step but Mrs. Mars, Darwin and Slim's mother. And she was wearing socks but no shoes.

This Easter, my ma had gotten it in her head that we should also learn a little bit about Passover; it had started when Mrs. Mars called her on the phone to buy some stamps. I only know because I had picked up the phone on the first ring upstairs and listened in on the whole thing. I admit it was weasely, but you can get away with it as you long as you don't huff into the phone too much.

"Hello?" my ma said.

"Oh, yes, hello, this is Mrs. Mars next door," Mrs. Mars whispered. "I was wondering if you had any two-cent stamps."

My ma and Mrs. Mars didn't talk to each other very much. That was weird all by itself, because my ma is a very interested person, and also pretty interesting. She's particularly nice to strangers, so she would have talked to Mrs. Mars a lot, if she had had the chance. But Mrs. Mars did not go out much, so it wasn't exactly like she met a lot of new people.

She's afraid of the weather, Slim said once when I asked him why his mother stayed indoors all the time. *She's just the same as anybody else, Digby; she just doesn't like it outside.* She was also nuts, but Slim couldn't really say that about his own mother.

My ma said, "Yes, I do have two-cent stamps, Gladys." She used her first name so Mrs. Mars knew she was friendly and not going to bite her, or cause bad weather to fall on her.

"Oh that's good. I wanted to send an Easter card to my sister."

My ma knew that Mrs. Mars was Catholic, and that Mr. Mars was Jewish. She also knew that their kids went to Catholic school, but not to Mass. But none of us knew if maybe Slim and Darwin were being raised as Jewish people.

"Oh, how nice. You must be busy getting your Easter dinner ready, then."

"No, no."

My ma paused, but she is not afraid to say things, so she just went ahead and said it.

"Will you be having Seder then?"

"Oh, no. Do you think I could buy three of your stamps?"

"Yes, yes. Anytime."

Mrs. Mars hung up, my ma hung up a little bit later, and then I hung up. Soon Mrs. Mars appeared at the kitchen door with a dime in her hand.

"I don't have exact change," said Mrs. Mars.

So, because she felt sorry for Mrs. Mars, and the Mars' religion, whatever the hell it was, my ma said that maybe we should find out what a Seder was. On Palm Sunday we had grape juice and lamb at dinner. My ma wanted to make it clear to God that we were still Catholic even if we were having an experimental Seder, which is why she made lamb, which is a pretty Catholic meat. We read the part in the Bible where everyone smeared blood on their doors, and there were also plagues around, but not right at that moment. My ma had the candle. It was kinda cool.

Mrs. Mars used to watch the Watergate hearings all day long while she was ironing. She was a walking encyclopedia on the small details, the really complicated stuff, and she was the first one to explain to me the difference between the break-in and the cover-up. My father never explained that to me.

Mrs. Mars always followed the same routine. She ironed during sentences, stretching out the pass of the iron to cover a long sentence, but then sometimes she slowed it down, and just worked on one wrinkled area while she waited for the words to stop. She only sprinkled water and flipped the clothes during pauses, when the senators shuffled their papers or looked over their glasses. During commercials, which didn't happen enough as far I was concerned, Mrs. Mars folded the clothes she had already ironed, and put hangers into Mr. Mars's shirts.

If it was quiet, you could still hear the iron *swusshing* in the basement, and the way it burped and hissed when Mrs. Mars set it back upright, like it was a little squirrel.

Darwin had been a talented cartoonist before he started doing pot, in the seventh grade. He had announced his retirement from illustration at the end of the school year. I was going to start fourth grade in the fall. I have one of his drawings here in my scrapbook: "Warlock Battles the Silver Surfer." The Silver Surfer holds his surfboard like a shield against a black jet-exhaust blast from the Warlock's left hand. Behind them are these tall buildings with yellow windows. Both the superheroes look gay, if you ask me. Still, I wanted to suck up to Darwin, basically because he had long hair and I was scared of it. So I tried to think of something to say to him when he gave the drawing to me.

"You drew this from scratch?" I asked Darwin after he handed it over. We were in his lab, which was his father's old shed, which was right next to his new shed. Once Darwin had brought out a broken television set that Mr. Mars was getting rid of. He put the TV in a trash-can and picked up a brick to throw through the screen. He had to wear heavy work-gloves, and he told me and Slim to stand back, because there was a vacuum inside the tube and it would try to suck us into it when the screen broke. We would be cut into little bloody pieces if we stood too close. I was scared of him, but he was also a god because he knew all kinds of gory stuff just like that.

When he tossed the brick in, though, there was just this thick *thud* and then some gray powdery dust. It was a letdown. Slim and I had been wrestling with each other to make the other one stand more in front, so he would be the one to get sucked into the vacuum.

"Me and another guy *created* it," Darwin said about the cartoon.

"Well, I like the—" I didn't really know what to say because I hadn't read many comic books—"The way it's arranged," I finally managed to blurt out.

Darwin was disappointed. He shaved down on his pinky nail gently with his pencil sharpener. "Rafe Biktor did the arrangement," he said. "I only did the inking."

"But the inking's pretty good," I went on.

"Yeah, it's not too shabby."

Darwin had a lot of posters up inside his lab. One of them was a picture of John Lennon in granny glasses squinting because he was looking toward the sun. Another poster was Pink Floyd, a picture of two guys walking toward each other with their hands out to shake, except one of the guys was completely on fire, even though he didn't seem to mind it very much. Darwin might be a yippie as well as a hippie. I'm not completely sure of the big dif between the two.

Mr. Mars was an inventor, or at least that's what Slim said. Everybody knew he really ran an electrical parts store in town, because we had all driven by the store a million times.

The story in our neighborhood was that if you were just a little kid, you could only stay up late enough on a Friday night to see Mr. Mars back out of his driveway and drive into town to his favorite bar. It was only when you were older that you could stay up late enough and hang around outside the Mars' house long enough to see Mr. Mars come weaving *back* from the bar. There was a telephone pole we kept praying he'd hit, but he never did. He always just missed it, and his Dodge Dart would creak on its suspension in the dip at the bottom of the driveway. We were cheering for him at the same time we were praying he'd crash, if you know what I mean.

Slim once explained to Emmet that Mr. Mars had told him that doctors had completely dissected a human body, and when they were finished analyzing every bit of it, they were able to say that they were completely sure there was no such thing as a soul, because they couldn't find it anywhere, so what did it look like?

Emmet spazzed out and went home crying to our ma. She said not to let it bug him, since Mr. Mars was Jewish and didn't have to believe in the same kind of soul as us. Mrs. Mars was Catholic, and it's barely even allowed for Jews and Catholics to get married. My brother asked where his soul was. My ma said, "Well, a little bit of it is in every little part of you."

Then Emmet started the litany—Is it in toenails and shouldn't we stop throwing them away? Is it in my clothes? I could see his little mind getting all sweet at the thought of it—Teeth? How about teeth? Is that why we get money for teeth?

Almost everybody in St. Tabasco seemed to come from nice houses that were pretty much alike. The kids I knew got enough money from their parents that they didn't seem to worry about money all the time, but it was hard to tell how much money a kid's father had just from the way the kid acted, since kids aren't supposed to have money.

But I knew that Mr. Mars was weird with money, and so were his sons, because he didn't make a lot. When he went to buy beer on Saturday, he took Slim with him because Slim had a pretty cool beer-can collection, but then Mr. Mars just bought a twelve-pack of Blatz and made Slim pay for any empty cans he wanted. The collection of empties were lined up behind the counter. And then Slim had to go with him to the bakery to buy two-day-old bread, and Mr. Mars flirted with the girls and asked them if they would ever date an older man. I knew about it because Slim told me.

I told Slim that was pretty sleazy.

"No, it's not," said Slim. "My dad's just different from your dad."

"How?"

"Well, he's not as mean."

"Bull," I said. That got me a little mad.

Mr. Mars was out of the house during the day. I said already that Slim acted like his dad was inventing a perpetual motion machine down at his second-floor shop in town, but that actually Mr. Mars just waited at the counter for people to bring in their busted appliances. Then he wrote them up a ticket and put new cords on appliances. Sometimes he just sent the stuff elsewhere to get fixed. That was about as scientific as he got. Although he did once show us a cool way to watch an eclipse, by looking at its silhouette through a pinhole. That way, he said, we wouldn't go blind like we would if we just stared straight up at it. I have to give him that.

When he came home at night, Mr. Mars sat in his recliner in the living room and read the paper. The recliner vibrated and had a warmer you could turn on in the headrest, even though Slim would spaz out if you changed too many dials. He always memorized the settings his father had made on the chair before he would let me sit in it. Then he would reset it when I was done futzing around.

When Mr. Mars read the paper, he sat hunched forward, as if he were ready to eject straight up into the air and fly away. He was not a very relaxed guy. He opened the paper wide and constantly snapped the pages with both of his hands, like he wanted to slap the news. And sometimes he mumbled and read things aloud, to nobody in particular.

I have been beat up before. You get beat up. You rest. And then you try to stand up. So there I was trying to stand up on the path, and Mrs. Mars had a grocery bag in one arm and a long old-fashioned black umbrella in the other, and socks on but no shoes. Some people said she was actually super-smart and had gone to graduate school, but other people said Mr. Mars kept her locked in the house without any money and wouldn't even let her go to the doctor. My ma said she was neurotic.

The poor woman.

My father said she's neurotic at best. Christ, they're both nuts over there. Our kids are gonna end up in asphalt barrels in their playhouse.

Mrs. Mars wore a man's raincoat most of the time when she went out. It must have been Mr. Mars's coat really, unless he just bought one for her that was a size smaller every time he went out to buy himself a raincoat. It looked like it fit her, but raincoats didn't exactly show your shape, if you know what I mean.

Mrs. Mars was wearing what looked like a lacy blouse underneath the coat, and she was skinny but also tall like a man. She had on a scarf, and a little bit of her hair was popping out from under the front edge of the scarf, so it looked like a horse's tail. Her cheeks were really red, but not like the nuns, who looked like they scraped theirs with brillo pads. Mrs. Mars's cheeks were a very healthy red.

She also always wore big, black rainboots. Mrs. Mars didn't like to be outside, I think, because she'd call from inside the screen door to Slim when she wanted him to come in. You could first see her elbow through the screen and then her shadow on the screen. She always had a rainhat on when she went out.

Mrs. Mars stopped and stared up at me. Then she said, "Ummmmmmm..." I turned away and waved backward with one of my twisted scratched-up hands, and then I walked down the street to my house.

Get In The Box

On the afternoon of January 3, 1975, I was only going to be home from school for a very short time, and I had to eat. And go. Then Slim and I were meeting Jake Myna. I stormed through the kitchen, grabbed a brick of cinnamon graham crackers, and kicked out high Hong-Kong-Phooey style, at Emmet's head, which was eating Velveeta cheese above the kitchen table.

Molly was also there, smushed into a chair, with her knapsack from pre-school still on her back. She was eating Cap'n Crunch and singing to herself very quietly. I could still hear her. She was saying, "Casper the friendly catholic." I swirled up the stairs. My ma called out my name from the basement, but I just screamed "Hi!" because I had to Go.

I went upstairs to the throne to go. I was reading, I was plopping, and I was still managing to eat graham crackers like a maniac. Cinnamon was drifting down from my hands through my lap. I thought about little bits of a lot of stuff. My guess was that Slim was already sitting out on our steps, making little gagging noises because I was late. I imagined that I could hear him all the way upstairs. It was the sound of him swallowing too often. He would never just come up to the screen and ask my ma to tell me to hurry up. Slim had to make it into a tragedy. Slim always acted like everything was fine, but his muscles would give his whole body a going-over. He'd much rather stand out in the middle of a beautiful afternoon, choking to death at the thought that Jake Myna was going to be pissed at us for being late.

Sure enough, when I finally finished and flushed and came back downstairs to the kitchen, my ma said Solomon Mars was sitting outside on the steps. I looked through the storm door and there he was, but he

31

was sitting sideways, so I knew he was watching out of the corner of his eye for anything interesting happening in the kitchen. His watch was on his right wrist and hadn't been off his wrist for more than three seconds since July of 1973. That's Slim. He knew down to the very last second what a big asshole he was.

Slim was so nervous that he was shaking the wrist of his left hand. The watch would slide up a little and then slide back down to where it is supposed to be. He'd do it twenty times in a row if he was really nervous. But then every time it slid back down, he had to look at it again, like he was checking to see if it was still working, as if each individual second might be taking a different length of time. The other thing he did a lot was stick out his chin and stretch his neck, like he was trying to get away from his collar. I know those were just nervous habits, and not his fault, but when you saw them as often as I did, you couldn't help but think that he was a pussy.

We were going to meet Jake for maneuvers. Slim Mars was terrified of Jake, so he wanted to be early. (I was only *afraid* of Jake, not terrified, so I wanted to be right on time.) Every time Slim came over, my ma invited him into the kitchen to wait, and he would always say no, and then sit on the concrete steps outside the kitchen, listening to everything but not participating.

I can tell you one thing, though. His parents have all these stuffy books about psychology and history and art jumbled together in one room next to their rec room, and Slim knows exactly where the book is that has a black-and-white picture of a naked woman with a wooden crescent moon tied to her face with a rope. He shows it to me every time we're over there, as if I've never seen it before. But it's not that I don't *want* to see it.

It wasn't like Slim was normal because everybody else in his family was weird. He was weird, too, because he just wanted to be normal. His older brother, Darwin, got started with all his science experiments because he was always fiddling around in their father's home shop, helping Mr. Mars fix stuff or just doing it himself. But Slim hated science. He went to the science fair because he knew I went every year, and he thought he was going to miss out on all the fun. Deep down Slim wanted to be a lawyer.

There was a new way of measuring things that Sister Ted was always threatening us with at school called the metric system. Some of it I understood, and some of it I didn't. The way I saw it, we had a different way of measuring things, but it wasn't good enough any more. We had to be like Europe and the rest of the world, so we'd all know what we were talking about when we sold each other stuff. In case we ever all became one big country. This is just so you'll understand how gay it was when Slim Mars tried to turn the metric system into a science fair project. Slim never tries very hard on his science projects.

The last friend I remember who was as embarrassing as Slim was named Hermie. When I was little, he and I went out to the street in front of his house once after dinner. We were screwing around trying to lift up the manhole cover off the sewer. The manhole covers were made out of rusted metal and they weighed a ton. They had these little raised hyphens on the top, and two little half-circle holes where you were supposed to put your middle fingers to lift them up. Hermie put his finger in one hole, and I put mine in the other. We could just barely lift it out, and then it would drop and echo like a gunshot in the sewer pipe beneath the street.

Then all of a sudden Hermie ran back onto his lawn and started climbing a tree. He didn't get very far up before he said "Aw, no!"

"What is it?" I said.

"I gotta go!"

"So?"

"I gotta go to the bathroom right now." Then he dropped trou fast as anything right there in the middle of the tree and started having the Hershey squirts. At first I laughed my ass off. Then I got grossed out. Hermie was crying so hard I figured I should go inside and get his dad. So I ran in and got him.

"Hermie's plopping in the tree."

Hermie's parents were watching TV in the kitchen. His father said "What?" but then he stood up like he had finally heard what I said, but a little bit later than when I said it. We went outside and stood underneath the tree.

"Hermie, it's okay. Pull up your pants and come on down."

"I don't want to! I want to stay up here."

"It's okay, son. I know you do. Nobody's mad at you."

"I had to!"

"I know you did."

"It came out!"

"I know it did, son." Hermie's father turned to me and said, "Digby, I think you better go home now." So I took off out of there.

Slim was afraid of Jake Myna because Jake made us do things and then run. The last thing we did was at Mr. Willard's house. Mr. Willard runs the florist shop in the middle of town. We lit highway flares in the street in front of Mr. Willard's house and he had almost had a heart attack. He seriously isn't as well anymore. Or at least that's what Jake said.

The second-to-last thing we had done caused Mr. Willard to beat the bushes around his house every night with his cane. We had wrapped a big mound of dog shit in some newspapers. Then Jake dropped it on Mr. Willard's doorstep and soaked it in lighter fluid. He rang the doorbell and dropped a match on the newspaper and then took off running back to where me and Slim were hiding in the bushes. Mr. Willard finally came out, but instead of stamping on it, he used his cane to pry the bundle open. When he saw what it was inside, he walked around his house whacking the bushes, looking for us.

The dog we got the shit from was a German Shepard named Peter. His dump was massive. He must have gotten into someone's garbage. This black guy who lives on our street owns him, but when you hear him calling for the dog to come inside it sounds like *Beat-a*! Peter has fleas so bad that he licks the outdoor electrical outlets on the house to try to fry himself and put himself out of misery. He puts his snout under the little silver cap and pops it open.

Jake was from a family of five—four boys, one girl. They were all tough. His father had been in the Marines and now he was a general contractor. All the boys went to a military high school. Jake wanted to go to West Point. He was already a good soldier. Everything he did had to have this organized side to it, where he was in complete charge and the other guys were slaves. He called Slim Mars and me "grunts." He was also a paramilitary freak and had mapped out the entire neighborhood's system of sewers so we knew how to crawl (really, we just walked stooped-over) from one street to the next street, without anybody seeing us.

One time Jake ditched me on Halloween. It bummed me out big-time. We had only been out trick-or-treating for an hour, and all of sudden, as we were crossing this big football field, he took off running, with Slim taking off right behind him.

I can't run very far or very fast, and Jake knew this, so he was deliberately ditching me. I was dressed as a football player, which was no big whup because it was football season, and I was wearing the uniform to practice every day anyway. Jake was dressed as a woman and had these little loaves of bread stuffed in a bra, which was pretty hilarious. Mrs. Myna had helped him get stuffed. She thought it was the funniest outfit she had ever seen. Slim was dressed as a cat, which was gay.

I ended up walking around the block a couple times and then going home early. I got in right after my ma got back from taking Molly and Emmet around our block, which was super early.

Emmet was dressed as a hobo, and Molly was a cat also, which made me laugh since I figured later I would tell Slim that and he would be burned for sure. My ma thought it was weird I was home so early, but she couldn't really say anything, because usually I would have been getting home too late, and she would have had to throw a fit the other way, so what was she supposed to do.

I always made sure to make up with Jake, because I had known him longer than anybody else in the neighborhood, and also because his younger sister Maxine had the largest boobs in my class at school. On the first day of eighth grade I gritted my teeth and walked right up to her.

"What's a nice girl like you doing in a hell-hole like this?" I asked, like a queer. It was not the greatest line, agreed. I had nothing ready. If I plan what I'm going to say that far ahead, I'll forget.

She laughed out loud, and then went like she was going to slap me. *That* might have been a sign that she was getting ready to make out with me. Hitting a girl is much different from hitting a guy. I acted like it was a big hoot, and got a whiff of her skin really close up. Baby-powder, Dial soap and watermelon—not a bad combo.

But then she baby-slapped my face, not hard, but I spazzed. Instead of kissing her, I twirled around and booted down the hallway, with a minimum of a half chub sticking out the leg of my pants.

My feeling was that first base would be nice to get first, though. They're in order for a reason. First base, to get a kiss, you just have to be fast. You can potentially kiss anyone. If you surprise someone by kissing them they can't kill you for it. They can just act mad, but it might be an act. Second is trickier. With a big girl, it seems to me, it's not much. Just hugging her probably counts as second for some. Third is where the word "private parts" comes from. It's tucked away, but it's basically an open wet hole, and a pretty busy area, too. I've heard there's more than one hole. Home base is, well, it's home base. Everybody comes out of the dugout to congratulate you. You get to rest for a while.

I used to go by the Myna's house at night and wait around outside. Sometimes I'd see her walk by the window in the living room, talking on the phone, looking outside, but it was always dark and she couldn't see anything outside. But I could see clear as a bell inside. In the fall it was cold out there but not too bad. I just shuffled around to keep warm. I had tried to build up my nerve (for what? I wasn't going to do anything). I whistled these five notes to myself over and over again:

Whistle while you work!

At the Myna's house, Maxine had to do her homework, but her brothers usually left their books by the front door and picked them up there again on the way back to the school in the morning. They were pretty smart to begin with, for being as good at sports as they were. You could always eat anything you wanted to there, any time you wanted it. Her mom also served meals from time to time, and you could also eat then, but it didn't affect your snacking just because a regular meal was coming up. If Mrs. Myna was fixing a casserole, and Jake and I wandered in, Jake might ask me if I wanted a hot dog.

Let's say that I said Yeah, which was pretty likely. Jake would scoot around, leaning in over and under where his mom was cooking, and Bam! he'd fix us a couple of hot dogs and make jokes the whole time, and his mom would just laugh like he was the cat's pajamas.

She'd only get mad really fast at Jake if he hadn't done something she had especially asked him to do, because his father needed it done. But she never stayed mad. Mrs. Myna had a great sense of humor, which was good because she needed to laugh a lot, and she also liked boys, which was also a good thing because they were everywhere in that house.

When we sat there eating our hot dogs, and Mrs. Myna finished cooking the casserole, she would offer us some of that, too, even if we were still chowing down on the dogs, or maybe she would just scoop it onto our plates without asking. Then she'd sit and smoke a cigarette and watch us eat, and maybe have a little dish of ice cream. The casserole would just sit there on a hot plate getting cold.

It was a crazy house, but it was fun. Now, in the kitchen at my house, you could only eat what was open, and most things you couldn't open, because they were for Everyone. And I could definitely not make my own meal while my ma was making a meal for Everyone. She would have looked at me like I was a loony tune. Jake never ate at our house, and I couldn't blame him. It would have been like a prison after his house.

Have your ever seen the TV commercial for Hebrew National Hot Dogs? Uncle Sam is standing way up in the sky like he's on stilts, and he's staring at a Hebrew National hot dog. God is talking to him from off-camera, in a real echoey voice. It tells about how Hebrew National doesn't care about health regulations for hot dogs, because they made them so great to begin with, because they had to answer to a higher authority. That means the Jewish God.

Uncle Sam is wearing make-up that makes him look like a cross between Abe Lincoln and Santa Claus. He has a pretty sad face to begin with, and he keeps looking sadder and sadder, because God keeps telling him how good Hebrew National Hot Dogs are.

They were good, too. They were beef. Regular hot dogs were made from pigs, who would eat anything. My father said that they would put almost anything into a hot dog these days, including head cheese.

"What's that?" I asked. I didn't know what.

"It's an unmentionable," he said.

"So why did you mention it?" I was being smart, since at first I was being dumb, by not knowing what it was. But then my father didn't answer me at all.

Sometimes I like to think about what the Hebrew National commercial would look like if they had made it at Jake Myna's house. Uncle Sam would be sitting at their kitchen table with his knees bunched up underneath his chin. Their kitchen table was really just a picnic table with a plastic tablecloth.

Mrs. Myna would be speaking to him in her high sing-songy voice from the sink, with her back to him. Uncle Sam would still be holding a hot dog in his hand, but this time Mrs. Myna would be telling him about how *she* only answers to a lower authority, and that she was sure her kids would eat *any* kind of hot dog, as long as it was shaped like a hot dog.

In the Myna version of the commercial, Uncle Sam would get a big smile on his face while Mrs. Myna talked on and on. He would look around the kitchen and realize what a nice, sloppy, anything-goes place it was, and how well his regular old Catholic hot dogs would sell there.

Also, if you wanted to go along with Mrs. Myna when she went shopping, you could throw whatever you wanted in the bag, and she would buy it, no questions asked. Including Scooter Pies.

Soon me and Slim were walking up to the woods behind the Episcopal Church. When we were younger, we called it the Jew Church, because it wasn't Catholic and we didn't know about any other religion, except Jewish. We were late. Jake loved it when we were late. It meant he got to think of a new way to punish us.

Back in the fall, we had stolen some plywood from a construction site and built a long narrow box out of it. We had stolen a big floral arrangement from the Jew cemetery (Baptist, actually) that was on the other side of the woods. We propped the flowers up outside the box.

When we got into the woods, we found Jake immediately because we knew where the box that we had built was. He had lit a little fire, so we followed the smoke just to be dramatic, even though the whole woods was only about fifty feet deep, and you could have thrown a stone from one end to the other, no prob. Jake just stared at us when we walked up to him. Then he shouted, "You're late!"

Slim looked at me, and then he wiggled his watch like he was saying, I have a watch so it wasn't my fault. But that stuff doesn't work with Jake.

"You've got a frigging watch, Slim; why don't you use it?"

"I do use it—," Slim said, but Jake cut him off.

"Excuse me?"

"I do use it, Lieutenant."

Once we were in the woods, we had to call Jake Lieutenant. He called us his grunts. He said that meant we were drafted, but that he went to college and then enlisted.

"You know what happens to me at school if I'm late for drill? I do push-ups until I can't raise my arms over my head. You two pussies probably can't even do a single girl push-up." That was not true, I thought to myself. I could crank out girl pushups, as long as I could get down on my knees for them, like a girl. "Get in the box," Jake hissed.

We crawled into the box, and Jake told us not to move around. Then he undid his belt and pulled down his dees and took a shit on the ground right at the box-entrance. Jake always had to go too far so we could be sure he was nuts.

Even then it wouldn't have been so bad, if Jake had just gone away for a while, but instead he sat down right outside the box, just looking at the trees. He started talking, and we had to listen to him, because we were trapped. Slim and I just lay there side by side in the box looking at the plastic tulips through the opening. I could smell the shit and smoke from the fire.

There was this Prell Shampoo commercial on TV, where a pearl was dropping down really slow through the green slime. The whole time it dropped, some guy was talking about how Prell was just the greatest news ever for your hair. Well, that was how time passed inside the box, in slow motion. And I felt like, even though I was still looking out through my own eyes, I was really much farther back behind them than I usually was when I saw stuff, so all the stuff happening looked smaller. I could see the pearl, but it was tiny, and it was almost impossible to see how much it was moving, if it was even moving at all.

Jake jabbered. I knew he was trying to sound like his father, who didn't hit him when he yelled at him. Jake's father just spoke in a quiet voice like he was embarrassed to be so disappointed in Jake. Then Mr. Myna started crying halfway through, which killed you, because he was such a big guy that you were expecting him to really punch Jake's lights out. It was really too bad he didn't.

Jake wasn't about to cry, but when he got wound up like this, it was like he didn't even need us there to hear him. He was just talking to himself about something only he knew about anyway.

While Jake was talking, I looked straight out at his dump and thought about making him eat it. But then I thought about myself eating it, which is always the problem with a thought like that. So then I checked out Slim's ear (which my nose was practically in) and thought about stuffing Jake's dump in there. Slim and I had to keep shifting around in the box to redo where our elbows were. Elbows were the main body part that didn't fit too well in that box.

Then I started thinking about the La Brea tar pits, where they found the bones of the saber-tooth tiger. It's in California. I don't why I thought about it right then, but I'm not lying.

I wondered how Hermie was doing now. It would be pretty sad if his dump in the tree was going to be the only thing I ever remembered him for, but everything couldn't be a Kodak Moment.

Home

My family would rather read than do anything else. It starts with my father but doesn't end there. My father always liked travel books, but I don't know much about them. I didn't *love* it here, where we lived. I mean, some days were better than others, but I don't know. I hadn't really been anywhere else except the seashore. That was nice. But last winter, in January, it got so cold and dead. You know, it was winter. It's probably what the rest of our solar system is like year round, but for me, it sucked big time.

Our house looked different from different angles. When I was cruising down the hill on the sidewalk, I couldn't see it, there where it sat at the bottom of the road, until the very last turn, because there was an angle in the road, this little jag, and also a bunch of high bushes in front of the house across the street. Then it jumped out at me, roof first, saving me from walking forever. It always turned out to have been up there ahead of me the whole time, just hidden.

From the backyard it looked humongous and white, like the side of a barn. It looked like someplace you couldn't walk right into, but would have to circle a few times to find the right entrance. From one side, the left, it looked like a chimney, because that's mostly what you could see. From the right side it looked like a little church with a pointed roof. From the air you probably wouldn't notice our house at all. For that matter, when I was inside it I didn't think about what it looked like, either.

You'd never be suspicious, just looking at the front of the house and the white curtains over the living room windows, what went on inside there. For instance, my little brother, Emmet, is really afraid of Siamese cats. There was one on the block with white-and-light-blue eyes and black fur, named Frank. Emmet thought that Frank waited around our house for him and then put a curse on him.

One time last year I came in the house through the front door and the living room was dark. Then I saw something moving on the sofa. When I turned on the light I could see it was Emmet. He had his knees on the cushions and he was looking through the front window. I thought he was playing the game where he made the living room into "the moon" by turning off all the lights and wrapping himself in the white curtains. But when I leaned over him and poked my head between the curtains, above his, I saw that Frank the cat was sitting right under the window looking up at us. I asked Emmet why he was so afraid of him.

"They're bad," he said, after thinking it over for about two years.

"What's so bad about them? They're cats. They were born cats."

"In that movie they sing a song," Emmet whispered. He started singing it really loudly.

"We are SiaMESE if you PLEASE! We are SiaMESE if you DON'T PLEASE!"

"Emmet, I know how the song goes."

Emmet was licking his lips now. "They don't care what we think. They don't CARE."

I was reading some more of this biography I had gotten out of the school library about Dr. Richard Drew. He was this incredibly smart black guy who discovered giving blood. Then he died in a car crash, because they wouldn't let him in at a white hospital, even though he was so light-skinned he barely even looked black. He didn't have anything left to worry about, because he just invented blood types and then died because white people were dicks, and stupid, because if they had helped him stay alive, who knows what he would have invented next?

There were only two black kids in my school. One was African and in the first grade, and the other one was in Emmet's class. Emmet said he was a bully, but Emmet said that about almost everybody, so you had to take it with a grain of salt.

Black stuff could be pretty smooth. There was one Black Power poem that was really cool, probably especially if you were black, but cool any-way even if you weren't. It was by W. E. B. Dubois, who was black:

I am the Smoke King.
I am black,
I am darkening with song.
I am hearkening to wrong;
I will be black as blackness can,
The blacker the mantle the mightier the man.

I didn't have a Dick Tracy lunch box anymore. Now I had a plain red plaid one (which I know was no great improvement, but when I went to high school I was going to use a brown paper bag.) Emmet's was Hong-Kong Fooey, and Maud carried a salad in a Cool Whip container. Molly's lunch box was bigger than her bookbag, and the thermos was a *silo.* Jesus Herbert Christ.

> Hong Kong Phooey! Number One Super Guy!
> Hong Kong Phooey! Quicker than the human eye!
> He's got style- a groovy smile and a bod that just won't stop!
> When the goin' gets rough, he's super tough with a Hong Kong Phooey chop!

Maud was annoying when she was eating, the type of person who was always acting like she was on a diet. When she ate an apple, she ate the entire thing, the seeds, the core, and the stem. Once I told her that that was retarded.

Maud said, "You're retarded. It's all part of the fruit. It's all good for you."

"Eat this," I said back. Sometimes, if you said a short thing after a long thing had been said to you, you won. It was almost as good as ranking on someone.

Maud also made open-faced tomato sandwiches with melted cheese, which were pretty great. She almost never made me one these days, but she used to.

When Emmet made his regular grilled cheese sandwiches, he acted like it was the most important religious thing he had ever done. He couldn't make them if anyone else was in the kitchen. The cheese had to be sliced into rectangles and put into a little pile. He sat and waited for the butter to soften, which he thought could only happen if he stared directly at the butter dish. Each side got thirty seconds exactly in the frying pan, and then he flipped. He timed it.

When we had breakfast at our house, it was the same thing every day. My ma was at the sink with a washrag or over the stove with the flipper. My father had already gone to work. He had one cup of coffee while he stood at the sink looking out at the backyard. It took one minute. He patted his pocket, went to get matches, and then he left.

The table had four cereal boxes on it, and we sat behind them reading them. The backs of the cereal boxes changed about once a month, but it always seemed to be the same thing: a giveaway contest where you had to send in proof-of-purchases, or a cartoon. When the back of the box you were reading did change, you could memorize the whole new thing in about three spoonfuls of cereal. But you read it again anyway every morning for two weeks. Then my ma would go to the store.

I read Sugar Smacks, Emmet read Puffed Rice, and Molly looked at her Cap'n Crunch box. Maud used to read Raisin Bran, but sometimes these days she tried to act like Victor Mature and read the newspaper and talk about it, but none of us talked back. I mean, *we* all still had our cereal boxes, and my ma hadn't even read the paper yet, so usually nobody could follow what Maud was talking about.

Molly is not too bad, so far, as a baby, but I can see exactly where she's working on being just as annoying as Maud is, when she gets older. Like at breakfast. Molly mumbles into her cereal like she is talking to each separate little piece of Cap'n Crunch. It drives me crazy, because it's already the worst to be hunched over the kitchen table at 7:30 in the morning thinking about Sister Ted's big mug floating down out of the orange juice to pick at my shirt and tell me my handwriting is sub-average.

"Uhm. Uhm. Uh ehh eh em. Uhm," Molly mumbles.

"Molly, could you not burp all over your cereal?" I ask her in my most brotherly voice. She smiles at me with all her teeth.

"Ohm. Em. Uh oh. Kay."

At my house there's usually no such thing as a simple meal. The roof always comes off a little any time we sit down to eat. The phone starts ringing, and the milk starts spilling out of the gallon jug (and usually directly into the butter dish). My father gets mad and somebody feels sick and somebody else won't finish his food and so the no-dessert-threat is made. Then the person does finish his food but says something wise.

All right, no dessert for you, smarty, my father will say to Emmet, lopping off a cube of butter, his thumb resting on top of the stick like it's the king of the hill.

You said I could get dessert if I ate three-quarters of my succotash, and I ate it. Didn't he say that, ma?

Don't pull me into this.

Like I said, no dessert for Mr. Know-It-All.

But you did say that, my ma says.

Am I going to get any support here?

I'm just saying you said it. (She is mad at him for touching the butter, which is what a slob does.)

We are one in the spirit, we are one in the Ford, Molly starts singing.

If I don't get to eat dessert, I'm going to spit up my succotash back on my plate.

You do that, Charlie, and you'll wish you hadn't.

But you said—

I don't care what I said *then*; I care about what I'm saying *now*.

Then Molly starts crying because she doesn't know the rest of the words to the song, and Emmet sticks himself with his fork, and Maud clears the table, and my ma hands out dessert, including to Emmet. I'm so busy watching that it is surprising that I can still shovel in as much grub as I'm shoveling.

I said he wasn't going to get any.

It doesn't seem fair—

But I *said* it!

Then Maud moves Emmet's plate, and it is discovered that he had transferred all of his succotash one spoonful at a time underneath it, and then smooshed down the plate. And then we all know he is doomed.

There was a New Deal in our house. Me, Emmet, and Emmet's homework. After my father's chore list bombed, I made this separate agreement with my ma that I would look over Emmet's homework every day, just to make sure he wasn't zoning out. In return I would get this lousy tiny allowance once in a while that made my ma think she was the most generous person in the universe. The chore list story is this: one day my father came home from work and announced that he had drawn up an allowance list. That was the good news. Up 'til then, every time any of us begged for a little money, he threatened that we were going to get regular allowances with assigned chores. When we had spent our allowances, we wouldn't be able to ask for any more money.

He handed the list to Maud.

"Why is Ma's name on the list?" Maud said.

"My name?" my ma said.

"Yeah, right here. You have to walk the dog."

Well, we all got a big laugh out of that, except my ma wasn't laughing.

"You've got to be kidding," she said. She looked at the paper, then balled it up and threw it in my father's face.

It ended up we got regular chores to do, but not regular allowances.

By the way, this deal with Emmet's homework had just started. I was getting five dollars every two weeks. My friend Jake Myna caddies for his dad's friends at the Myna's club, and they all tip him incredible amounts of money and let him drink beer after the ninth hole. My friend Solomon "Slim" Mars gets a big allowance from his grandmother which he keeps in his own bank account, like a homo.

Every night we had to go into our rooms for at least an hour with the door closed. And they watched our report cards. Cs meant you were grounded for a while, automatically.

Since Emmet was just finishing the fifth grade, he got some unbelievably stupid weird homework assignments, since in fifth grade the nuns weren't even convinced that kids know how to do anything. Emmet was a genius in some ways, but mental in some other ways.

The thing with Emmet was that he was very quiet and serious about everything stupid, but he treated everything like a joke that was supposed to be serious. This is the complete opposite of me. So helping him out with his homework was like trying to stomp out my own shadow as if it was on fire. It was impossible. I never really knew if I was getting through to him or not, so I was probably not. It was one more reason why I couldn't wait to get into high school. I wouldn't have to help him any more. Molly didn't really get homework. She brought home pictures she drew in kindergarten, and we were all supposed to make a big deal about it. Emmet made the biggest deal of all.

I can't stand helping Emmet with his homework. I'm ready to do my own stuff, and I have to stop. I look across the kitchen table at Emmet, who is staring straight ahead over the Velveeta cheese block in front of him. There are little nibble marks around the edges of the cheese. That was something I could not have gotten away with. I would be screamed at in one of the following ways:

Get a knife!

Or—

Stop acting like you live underneath a rock!

I was always arguing with my parents that I should be treated like Emmet, and that Emmet should be treated like me. It got complicated when I was trying to explain to them how unfair it seemed, so I almost always gave up. Usually I was just trying to tell them that I felt bad.

"Where's your bookbag?" I asked him. Emmet opened up his eyes wide when I asked him, which meant his bookbag could be any place. He reached into his pants pocket and pulled out some mimeographed pages.

"That's it, that's all your homework? Where's your bookbag?" I was waiting for my ma to turn back around to the sink, so I could jab him really quick, so he would know we were getting down to business.

"Digby! That's Emmet's homework right there," my ma said. "Don't torture him about his bookbag. You know, some day you're going to have to start treating him like a human being." When she finally turned her back, I looked at him and thought, Over my dead body. Then I made a small claw out of my right hand and raked it down Emmet's forearm very lightly. He closed his eyes tight.

"This should only take a minute," I said. I yanked the papers out of his hand and kneeled down by the table. "I remember this assignment. It's a breeze." I said this to Emmet about all of his homework even if I didn't know what the hell it was. That way he'd believe me five minutes later when I said we were all finished.

I slapped the purple mimeographed pages around, and I put my elbows on either side of the top sheet to keep them in place. It was a vocabulary review, where you had to match words with definitions. Emmet had already started it, connecting the word *anxious* to the definition *troubled, worried, wishing very much.*

"This is good, Emmet, that you started this already. That's real good," I said to him.

I wanted my ma to see that I had started out on the right foot. I would be able to help Emmet finish quickly as long as he didn't go wacko on me.

Emmet didn't say anything. Ninety-nine times out of a hundred, Emmet will not say anything at all. He took out this incredibly thick ball-point pen that could write in ten different colors, depending on how many times you clicked the button at the top. I hated that kind of pen. Half of the colors were always dry, but it was Emmet's holiest possession, and he wouldn't leave for school in the morning unless it was in his shirt pocket.

I slid my finger down the left-hand margin to the next word.

"Business. Now what's the definition that fits *business*? He worked his pen down the right side of the page where the definitions were, and stopped at *occupation, thing one is busy at*. We worked for about five minutes and finally got to the last word on the list. It was "despair." Emmet nailed the right definition. *Loss of hope.*

I was going to be fourteen. Emmet was eleven and still wore a night-cap to sleep, for God's sake; Molly was six; and Maud was a year older than me but you wouldn't know it. And then there was my ma and my father. My mother was mean but had a sense of humor, but my father was just mean.

My ma always said, He's not mean, he just has a bad temper. She smiled when she said it, but it wasn't the greatest joke.

In my scrapbook, from December 1, 1967, there is a note I wrote to my father: "Daddy I *Think* you are The best Daddy in The World." (I didn't sound very sure.) I circled "To Daddy" on the front of the sheet, with a circle about as big as a dime.

That was the last time I liked him. It seemed that way sometimes. I got him a book on Lindbergh for his last birthday, and he acted like he was going to read it, but then he went back to reading *The Voyage of Kontiki*. I know because I saw that book in his briefcase. I read a quote inside the Lindbergh book. It was the note they found on his nightstand when he died in his sleep: *I know there is infinity beyond ourselves. I wonder if there is infinity within.*

His briefcase didn't have much in it, usually just two packs of cigarettes and two or three paperback books, his reading glasses, a nail-clipper, and a little bunch of cards and pieces of paper rubber-banded together with phone numbers and addresses on them. Sometimes there was also a yellow legal pad in there.

My father didn't bring work from the office to do at home, like Mr. Myna, or have part of his shop at home, like Mr. Mars, and he came home on time. You could set your watch by what time he came home. Sometimes he had a brown bag under his arm, sometimes not.

My father like to read about different places around the world. He said he didn't want to go to them, but he liked to know everything about them even if he never got there. He liked characters in a book second, and how the places were described first.

Back to *The Voyage of Kontiki*. I think there was a picture on the cover of a guy and a girl doing it, with a lion behind them also. (But not doing it with them.) I'm not exactly sure. I only saw it from a distance. My father was reading a section about trees, and he stopped and looked at me, and then kept going on about the tree business, as if he was still reading, but he really wasn't. It was confusing. I had been staring at the cover, but not really looking at it.

My father said, "All the trees aren't like that, though. There's one gray dead tree as wide as a small circular room. There's jagged cracks all shot through it and you can step inside it."

"What, have you been there?" I said. I mean, that's what it sounded like.

"I have not been there, pinhead."

There were other ways my father was not like other fathers in our neighborhood. He wasn't very coordinated, not that I should talk. He got the shakes when we were punching around, playing got-you-last, and I threw him a half-assed head-fake. And he shook if he tried to throw a ball. He also didn't go to church anymore. He didn't even look at my ma when she stared at him on Sunday mornings, when everyone else was getting dragged out to 11:15 Mass.

Once I tried to argue that *I* should be allowed to stay at home from Mass, too.

"You're not staying home," said my ma. I knew she meant it, and that was that. But I had to say some crap about it.

"Ma, don't you think that a kid should get his religion from both his parents?

She looked at me. My father should have defended me if I was right, but he didn't, so she had to let me get away with some wisecracking. She might have been mad at him, but she felt sorry for me. That was a problem in our house. Everybody had to do opposite things at the same time a lot.

I tried to listen to my parents sometimes, not to obey them, but to hear if I could tell what they really meant. If my father said, You have to take out the trash now, I knew that he knew I knew when trash night was. Trash is one of my chores. Still, I knew when trash night was. When my father tried to tell me, I knew he meant something else, but I couldn't tell him that I knew that, and I didn't know what the something else was.

My ma got a patient worried line on her forehead when she had to really answer something we asked her, and she sighed a lot as if it were hard work to give a good answer. But that doesn't tell you too much about her. I can describe what she looked like, because sometimes people look like what they really are, but the best way to describe what my ma was really like is by describing her purse, since it weighed a ton and she kept everything in it that she needed. My whole family was stranded once by the side of the road when our car broke down on the way to the beach, and we survived on my mom's purse for five hours.

We found batteries, a red scarf to tie on the antenna, dried fruit packages, three rolls of quarters, four small memo notebooks, three combs, some dried pasta, an extra pack of my father's cigarettes, two compacts, a lot of paper clips, and a hardback book. I can't remember the other stuff, but I know there was more than that.

If you could put your head in her purse you would feel like you're right up close next to her. It smelled of her perfume and her powder and her lipstick. There was one mound of clean Kleenex, and also a separate piece that had a print of her lips on it, from when she was blotting. She had very full lips. They looked like two mustaches, one on top of the other, except they weren't hairy and dark, like most mustaches, so maybe that doesn't help you too much.

She had almost no gray hair at all. When she did grow one, she made all of us look at it with her.

"I want you to see what you're doing to me," she said. The next day, if somebody asked to see it again she would say that it had disappeared, and maybe it did. Maybe she pulled the hair out herself and flushed it.

Her nose is big. Maud has her nose, because hers is also big. My ma says it is a genius nose, which means only smart people have them. Her eyes are also very big, which makes you think she's always surprised, but she's not always. They're just big all the time. Her fingers are long and very skinny, almost like little legs with clear square boots on the bottom of them.

Miss Twinkletoes

I eat a lot of candy, but it's nothing compared with how I used to eat last year. I'm still getting bigger all the time. Around my waist there's a tire, like you forgot to take the air-hose off. I'm starting to get these tiny zits on my chin that are ugly. My ma will say, Oh, you're getting a bump, when she sees them, but she's not kidding me a bit with that bump stuff. They're zits, filled with white crap. My father had acne when he was young. He still has scars on his back. I've seen them.

I'm addicted to the lunch I bring to school. In fact, sometimes I tell Sister Ted I have to get another pencil out of my bag, and I go back in the middle of the morning to the cloakroom, stick my head between the coats and lean over my knapsack, and eat half my sandwich in one bite. We get three sheets of smoked turkey on white bread with mayo. That is so little meat that I can breathe it right down, almost without chewing. George Gack gets the whole pack of meat on his sandwiches, since he's an only child. He makes the sandwich himself. It's quicker for him just to flip the whole stack of meat right onto the bread than it is to peel it away, one sheet at a time. Sometimes I eat so fast I don't even remember eating. But if I eat slow, food tastes funny, like when I'm reading and I stare at one word too long, and it starts to look ridiculous, like the word "the."

The the the the the the the the the the the the the the the the the the the the the the the the the the the the the the the the the the the the the the the the the the the the the the the the the the the the the the the the the the the the the the the the the the the the the the the the the the the the the the the the the the the the the the the the the the the the the the the the the the the.

At school that day they were making the usual to-do about who the science fair judges were going to be. There was a priest who used to teach chemistry in high school about fifteen years ago, and also one of the nuns, but not Sister Ted, thank God, who would rather have her head chopped off than hand me a ribbon, and an engineer named Ray Lasher, who happened to be Ray Lasher Senior, the father of the evil Ray Lasher Junior.

Ray Lasher Jr. had been in my homeroom every year for eight years. For seven straight years we had faced each other in the science fair. Where I looked crusty, Ray looked shiny. He had dark black hair that waved around on his head like it was looking for a nice place to land. His eyes were brown and he was lean and strong, and always the fastest, first, and farthest in every gym class. And since homerooms always took gym class together, I always got to see him do it the best, whatever it was. And It was a lot of things.

I hated his hair and his head. I hated his clothes and the way that he swung a golf club like it was the lightest thing in the world, and all he had to do was to give the ball the slightest touch to send it rocketing through the air to the middle of the fairway. I hated the way teachers said his name, Raaay, when he was acting up in class, because they said it with little smiles on their teacher-mouths that meant that things some kids did wrong were funnier than when others did them. And he always smiled because everything always went his way.

So Ray Lasher Junior made me nervous enough. I didn't want to have to face his father, too. Not to mention the time over the summer that I caddied for Ray Senior at the country club. He had gone into the clubhouse, after nine holes of making fun of me for being a lard-ass, to have a drink. He came out, made fun of me for nine more holes, and gave me $6.10. $6 is the minimum they have to pay, so he only tipped me a dime, like a fink, considering that his bag was as heavy as a torpedo, and that I got poison sumac on my legs from searching in the woods for all his duffed balls in deep brush. If I found one, I'd try to hand him an iron to dig himself out with, and he'd just walk right past me, and then say over his shoulder, I think the foot-wedge is the right club for this shot, caddy. Don't you? Then he'd kick the ball back out onto the fairway.

If you're going to have the most expensive clubs in the world, and all those accessories, for God's sake you should be able to hit the ball. He was hopeless. I stared at his stupid white shoes that looked like they had a bib on them. I didn't even look at Lasher's face when he came over to get a club out. He was that bad.

But the joke was on him, because when he took that break after the first nine holes, I ordered five dollars worth of food instead of the one soda we were allowed. I heard that he came out cursing like a madman when he went to pay his greens bill and found out what his caddy refreshment tab was, but by then I had vamoosed to the caddy shack to hide. I was hungry after walking around for two hours in the sun with a bag on my neck full of golf clubs! I already said I'm getting bigger all the time. Big guys get hungry. If you're smaller, of course, you might not. You can probably survive for a full week on an apple or some crackers. But I get so hungry I get angry. Sometimes I want to walk up to the Keebler Elf tree and knock on it, and when one of the Elves sticks his little green cap-head out through the tree-hole, I want to grab him by the neck and shake him like a toy-dog, until he comes up with some free cookies for me.

Lasher caught up with me later, though, in the parking lot.

"I got my eye on you, Shaw, and I don't like what I see. I think you don't have any balls. You got any balls, boy?"

I didn't really think that was something I had to chat with anybody about, because I have seen my own balls and that's good enough for me, so I didn't say anything to him. My father doesn't ever play golf. He doesn't even have any friends who play golf. Come to think of it, I don't think he has friends.

Luckily, there was also usually somebody else judging the science fair, who had nothing to do with science at all, called the "Layman Expert." That was to make sure that even dummies could understand what you were talking about.

This year, just like last year, it was going to be a second grader's mother, Mrs. Vaughan, because she didn't work during the day and liked to read science fiction. She loved me because I talked to her about her shoes. She was wearing Dr. Scholls the day of the fair. Dr. Scholls were these wooden sandals where your toes went into a scooped-out section in the front.

She walked up to judge my enzymes project and put out her hand to lean against the table my exhibit was on.

"Ooo, this shoe is killing me," she cried. She told me Dr. Scholls were designed to exercise the foot. "The toes are supposed to be able to stretch out and flex below the foot! But I think I'm being maimed by them," she added.

"That would make a pretty good science project itself," I said.

"Excuse me?" Mrs. Vaughan said.

"Somebody should study whether or not Dr. Scholls actually do what they're supposed to do, exercise the foot."

Mrs. Vaughan looked at me and smiled. There was a little bit of orange lipstick on her front teeth. "You seem to be a bright young man," she said. "Let's see. Enzymes? Well, that's interesting. What can you tell me about the little devils?"

I was glad she'd be judging again this year since we were old buds.

It turned out in the end that Mr. Lasher was replaced as a science fair judge because they miraculously scored this blind scientist from the National Institutes of Health. He was very famous. He couldn't see my horrible paint job or any of my typos. He liked my title: *ARTIFICIAL FERTILIZATION IN A LOWER ANIMAL: A VIRGIN BIRTH,* and kept saying it to himself after I told him. He had said that I was unafraid to follow through on a valid experiment, even if it wasn't popular.

Mrs. Vaughan liked it, too. She stopped by and said that my project was politically important, that I was suggesting that women's bodies are like their own laboratories, and that it was a good thing for control of that particular lab to be given back to them. Not a bad speech for a housewife with orange lipstick on her teeth and mutilated toes.

It was nice to have somebody believe in me, even if the whole believing-in-you thing can be a lot of baloney. Most of the time someone older says it to you, to force you to do something.

I believe in you.

You do?

Yes, I do. I believe you will do the right thing.

How will I know if it's right or not?

You just will.

In eighth grade, you felt like a king inside your own head and your own school, but once you were outside it everybody was older than you. And since you weren't even in high school, they ruled out whatever you said automatically as being immature. It was like you weren't alive yet, you were just saving a place in line for someone who was going to get there eventually, and that person was you, only when you were older.

Everybody was pretty excited at recess, but not because of the science fair. That night was going to be the second Ali-Frazier fight. All the guys in the eighth grade were making bets on it. I even made a bet on it. I'm very cheap about betting because it's hard to win. I was taking Frazier this time, because the first time I had taken Ali and he had gotten whupped. Speaking of bets, when Evel Knieval jumped the Snake River Canyon, a lot of the eighth graders bet that he was going to die. He really wanted to jump the Grand Canyon, but that was a national park, so it was no-can-do. Plus, that would have been too far to jump. Evel didn't even make it over Snake River, but he floated down in a parachute and only broke a couple of ribs, which was not too bad.

I was betting my friend Fitz Patrick and was trying to have some common sense. I figured Frazier was the better fighter, since he had won the first one. I only bet four dollars. Fitz Patrick was very cool, and once his father had taken him to a prize-fight, even though it hadn't been heavyweights, only bantamweights. He told me I made a good bet, so that was something. But most of the eighth grade seemed to be going for Ali, which scared me.

I had stolen the four dollars from my ma's purse. You can pinch sixteen quarters between your thumb and first finger easily. It's only a little more than an inch of a stretch. I can dip into her purse and be out in a split second, not that that's something I should brag about.

After school I walked home and went downstairs to do some homework. Ultraman, using the old Beta capsule, was about to transform himself and kick some serious butt. It turned out I had already seen the episode before, but I always had the TV on when I was downstairs. Why else go down there? I also had the "W" World Book open on my lap, and I was copying the section on Henry Wallace word for word, because we were studying the 1948 Presidential elections in social studies, and I had to give a speech the next day, while my cool teammates giggled and passed notes behind me that were probably about what a spaz I was.

I always do my homework in front of the TV. It's less boring that way, but sometimes it gets confusing. On that particular day, my brain wandered off into a weird cloudy world where Henry Wallace was shooting electrical bolts shaped like circular saw blades out of the side of his hand, and Ultraman was the one shaking the hands of regular old Americans who worked with their own hands and still could never make enough money to own anything. Ultraman shook their hands, and asked them in Japanese if they would vote for him. It was a dream, so it wasn't a big deal that now I could understand Japanese all of a sudden.

When you get up to turn off TV after you've been watching for a long time, the set is really hot. On the old TVs, when you turned it off, the picture collapsed into a little white spot that kept getting littler and littler, and then you couldn't see it anymore, but it seemed like it was probably still there somewhere. You just couldn't see it because you were finished watching TV for that day. When you went outside, the sunlight felt fake.

That night after dinner my ma drove me downtown to the Library of Congress, because I had to find this old book from 1903 written by a guy named Jacques Loeb. I needed it for my science fair project research. I was going to make a sea urchin's eggs reproduce without fertilization. Old Jacques was the guy who first did parthenogenesis on sea urchins, the one whose experiment I was planning on stealing. The school librarian had called around and found the book for me at the Library of Congress. It was the only place in our whole area that had a copy of it.

I had been nervous about going to the Library of Congress, so I'd laid out everything I'd need ahead of time for going. That way I could practice like I was already there. I had my slide rule in its little plastic holder, with my name on it on a little piece of plastic tape. I put labels on everything I owned with this little gun that had the alphabet on a little wheel. You dialed up each little letter and then squeezed the trigger. *That* was practical.

The slide rule was so I could warm up a little on it before I took notes. I had only learned how to do square roots, multiplication, and division on it, but it was possible to do a ton of other stuff, like trig and calc and vectors. I had no idea how to do them, but I kept the booklet. The slide rule was also good for giving someone like my sister Maud a chop if she got in your way. I almost killed her with it once. She still has a tiny scar that looks like a checkmark underneath her right eye where it scratched her.

I had put a pocket protector in the shirt I was going to wear so I wouldn't ruin it by putting my pen in without a cap on it. The protector would still get ruined, no matter what. I also put a Texas Instruments calculator in my bag. And I brought a book of chess problems, just to have a book. You should always have a book with you.

My ma was pretty good about helping me with stuff like this.

You have a good brain and you're not going to toss it away like an old pair of pants, she told me.

I don't do *that*, I said back to her. I actually *do* do that, but you have to fight back.

You don't have any common sense. I'm saving your brain. It's the only thing that will ever get you anywhere.

Having a brain means I remembered a lot all the time, that it never shut off. The worse things get, the more I remembered. If I had common sense, I would remember just what I needed to remember and get along okay. It would be like a little bit of oil that lasted a long time.

The Library of Congress was almost as big as the Capitol Building. My ma and I walked into a huge central round room that had millions of little desks and chairs, and balconies way up high, near the roof. I had to look up the Loeb book in a thick card catalog, and write down all the information about it on a little card. Then I gave it to this librarian guy with big frizzy hair, who had a green Afro-pic in his pocket, but he was white. He told me to sit down since it was going to take a while. Then he put the card in this little round tube, and put the tube into a chute, which sucked it up into a pipe. Whuushh!

For the next half-hour my ma and I whispered about what other people might have been reading, based on what they looked like. We also did some worrying about getting caught whispering. Then a little elevator behind the librarian's desk clanged open, and the librarian took a small book out that had the card I filled out stuck to it with a rubber band. The librarian looked at it and called out my name, and I got my book. I made a copy of the pages I needed so I could read them at home. My ma fished some change out of her purse. She didn't say anything about the half of her quarter roll that was already missing, which at that very moment was in the process of being doubled, since Frazier had already broken Ali's jaw and went on to win by a unanimous decision, the first and last bet I ever won. Instead of paying up, Fitz offered to let me peep on his sister when she was changing clothes, which I had to admit was better than eight bills.

On the way home from the Library of Congress, we stopped at Hot Shoppes.

"We'll just get a little something," my ma said. She had an ice cream sundae, and I had a small fries and a piece of blueberry pie. The fries had to be fought over, because I was too hungry, as usual, and fries somehow made it a meal, instead of just a snack.

"We had dinner at home," my ma said. "Why don't you just get the pie, and see if you're still hungry after that?"

"I know I'm that hungry," I told her. "I didn't have much dinner." I said this not really believing that she would believe me, but my ma looked guilty, like it was her fault for not cooking a big enough dinner, so she let me get both. Then it turned out I felt guilty for making her feel guilty, and I also was completely stuffed, so I felt disgusting. But I still had to act happy as a clown.

We talked about my science project. I told her I wanted to be a scientist and that's why I catalogued and saved everything, and also why I had to test everything, because there was the scientific method that had rules you had to follow. One of the main rules was that you had to be empirical: you had to test things and you had to pay attention to the results. I could see she was listening to me at the very beginning, but then she looked like she was getting ready to talk.

Sometimes my ma tries to talk to me, but I don't want to, and other times I try to talk to her, but she doesn't want to. And sometimes she just can't hear what I'm saying. Like that time I got roped into being "Miss Twinkletoes" at the Cub Scout magic show. She wouldn't let me get out of it. Some of those guys STILL think I'm gay because of it and I was only nine years old then. On the night of the magic show, my ma dragged me into the bathroom at the public elementary school where we had our meetings. All the parents and brothers and sisters of all the Cubs were out there. My father was outside having a cigarette when we were in the bathroom. My ma put red lipstick on me and a blonde wig, and I wore my sister Maud's plaid skirt and white blouse. And high heels. I tried to argue with her, but I could hear the people arriving for the show, and their voices made me feel a little sick but also excited. I was peeping out the bathroom door and one of the other Cubs saw me and gave me the finger and I gave him the finger back, and the gold bracelet on my wrist flashed at him.

I ran out into the audience and squeezed my father's biceps when the magician needed a volunteer. I tried to pull him to his feet so he would come up and hold one end of the rope for the rope trick. I tried to pull him but he wouldn't budge. I had seen him laughing so hard he had to press a handkerchief to his face. (Maybe he was crying because his son was going gay wacko in front of his very eyes.) If he was laughing that hard, I figured he would get up and come with me and be the volunteer. I jumped on to his lap and put my arm around his neck, and he got this bug-eyed look on his face and started coughing. He pushed me off his lap, and I fell on the floor. The parents stopped laughing, but the kids kept going. My father sounded like he was choking to death.

I gave up and went back on stage, but all of a sudden the joke seemed dumb. I could hear the magician asking me in this serious voice, "Miss Twinkletoes, would you be so kind as to produce the silk handkerchief?" It seemed to take me forever to pull it out, because I was watching my parents, and a bunch of heads in the audience had turned to look at them, too.

The magic show was more than four years ago. But that was the last time I was a complete dumbass. Up until then I thought it was just that my father had a pretty bad temper, and that he only got it at night, when he came home from work, after dinner, on days he brought home his briefcase. If he yelled too much at my ma, and Emmet started crying in his bed in our room, sometimes Maud would come in and rub Emmet's shoulders and tell him it was okay. Then she would leave and Emmet would ask me questions.

Why does he get so mad?

Because he's Irish. Irish people have bad tempers.

Is he going to hit her?

No.

How do you get a bad temper?

I didn't really know, so I'd make something up.

You get a bad temper if your face gets really red really easily, and you're Irish.

When I was Miss Twinkletoes I finally saw that that was all bullshit. We were waiting in the living room for my ma to come downstairs so we could go. The news was on TV about Kent State. My father's briefcase was under the piano. The snaps were not fastened, and it had popped open. He used to come home from work and have a cocktail in a lo ball glass with painted bubbles on it. Now he still drank but you never saw it. Maud told me what it was called later on but it was at the magic show that I knew.

My father said, "The hippies can cry all they want to. They're not going to end the war. It'll probably still be going on when you're draftable."

"How old do you have to be to get drafted?" My ma was coming down the stairs.

He said, "You can go to war when you're sixteen, if your parents give permission."

"Not this again," my ma said.

"The Army was the best thing that ever happened to me."

She looked him straight in the face and said, "Ha!"

Now the war is supposed to end pretty soon. We're pulling out.

That night with my ma at Hot Shoppes was different. Both my ma and I were ready to talk. I was excited about my project. My ma was excited because we were alone and doing a project together, and also because we were getting to have a snack together instead of her just setting out the snack for me and then having to watch me inhale it like a big dog. So we both wanted to talk, but at first I couldn't really understand what she was saying about my father.

What I am talking about is the Vague Speech.

"You kids don't know. But sometimes I think I am going to have to go away for a little while."

"What don't we know?"

"It doesn't mean that I don't want us all to be together."

"I know he's an alcoholic," I said.

My ma almost dropped her spoon. "Who told you that?"

"I just know."

"Well, do you know what that means?"

"Yes." But I was praying she wouldn't ask me for a definition. I knew it meant he drank too much, but since I didn't drink at all, I had no idea how much was too much.

This was why I avoided really talking to my ma, because it always got really serious and sad before it had the chance to get anything else. When I wanted to talk to her it was because I wanted her to hear about what I was thinking, even if it was stupid, just because I thought she might be proud to hear me talk, as if I were a two-year-old who had just learned how to say "cat." But she took it personally, like we should change something about life every time I said something.

Maybe they will get divorced. My father is always fiddling with his wedding ring, but he never looks at it when he's doing it. It's almost like he's looking at one thing, way off in the distance, that he can adjust by tweaking another thing right at his fingertips.

He and my ma don't talk about their wedding. There's some old black-and-white pictures of them stuffing cake into each other's mouths, but that's about it, and as usual with a stunt like that, my father looks happier about it than my ma does. She looks happy, but happy-to-be-in-a-picture happy, not a happy-to-have-cake-stuffed-in-her-mouth happy. My father just looks happy.

We got home and things went regularly. I thought everyone had gone to sleep. I had already fallen asleep once watching the headlights on the ceiling that squeezed in over the curtains when a car whizzed by. Then I woke up, because I heard my ma talking to my dad very clearly.

"I want to talk to you about your drinking problem," she said.

"I don't want to talk about it."

"Well, I do," my ma said. She was not going to not say anything anymore. You could hear it in her voice. I could hear Emmet opening his eyes in his bed across the room. I could hear Maud lying on top of her quilt with her hands on her stomach listening. I could hear my little sister, Molly, stop sucking on her third finger.

"I'll just stop," my father said.

"You won't just stop. Try to think of the children."

"They don't know a thing about it."

"They do. Digby told me tonight that he knew you were an alcoholic.

I think Maud knows too. Don't you want to try to stop now before it gets too late?"

"It's not going to be too late. I can stop any time I want to. You'll see. I'll just stop now."

I grinded my face into my pillow until I saw stars, and I could hear blood pounding down my ears. My face smashed the pillow. In the dark now, with the house asleep, I could think about whatever I wanted. I thought about butting my head against a wall; in the dark I could almost see what it would look like if my hands tried to tear my face, my aching hands on the pillow.

I felt guilty for trying to be smart with my ma. I felt guilty for eating the fries. If you had to try to be smart you ended up dumb. You tried to be funny and everyone looked like they would cry. Jacques Loeb was smart. Muhammed Ali was funny. I was just Miss Twinkletoes.

Sister French
Conks Out

Catholics are so cheap that sometimes they don't even get real substitute teachers to cover for people, like when Sister French went off her tree. Instead, they got my ma, of all the people in the universe. She didn't like it very much either. She knew half the snotty guys in my class already, and so they felt like they could say anything to her, or do anything they wanted to do during class. It was because she was the mother of someone they knew, and not a real teacher, or at least not a nun.

My ma did like writing my report card, because she knew she'd be the only one to read it on the other end. She wrote little jokes to herself in the comments area, about how she just knew I could improve, if I would listen to my mother.

Sister Ted handed out things called Holy Corsages if she wanted to reward you but didn't feel like spending money and getting you a real gift. We were spending a week putting together an enormous one for Sister French after her conk-out, when she had gone back to Cincinnati to the convent. Sister Skeletona made an announcement the next day that Sister French had gotten sick.

"It was in her own interest to return home for a while," Sister Skeletona said. It was a weird thought, that a nun had a home. Monsignor Bronk wanted to make Cissy Snodgrass write an apology letter to Sister French, too, but her parents came in and had a conference, and Cissy said that her parents said Sister French was loco and it wasn't her fault she couldn't control herself.

For a Holy Corsage, Sister Ted usually counted up an entire class-room of students and got the girl in the class with the fanciest handwriting to write up a little scroll that said something like, *The Second Grade homeroom number 5 presents Digby Shaw and Peter Kiernan with a Holy Corsage of 25 Masses and 25 Holy Communions.* We got a Holy Corsage for selling cokes at lunch, but we had to split it. Then the second grade class was dragged to a morning Mass where they had to send up all of their holy thoughts about me and Peter to God, who would notice it and write it down, and then we would be blessed, and so on.

Crossing guards and traffic patrols got them. Students who cleaned up the yards after recess got them. Altar boys and the girls who sold supplies got them, and Fernando Huegros constantly got them on Friday after he had waxed the floors in the hallways every Thursday night. Sometimes we sent them home to our parents on holy days. Sister French got a whole school Holy Corsage—400 Masses and Holy Communions and Confessions and Rosaries, which was the biggest one since we had sent a humongous one to Monsignor Bronk on his 65th birthday, along with a key chain that had a picture of his pet canary on it.

Occasionally Sister Ted got one for herself, by suggesting to her brown-nose posse that they award some to the *other* teachers in the eighth grade. She let the goodie-goodies then have the bright idea themselves of also making one with *her* name on it.

Sometimes the scrolls had the little postage stamp-size pictures of every kid in the whole class on them, and you had to write *Thanks for being a patrol* or whatever you were thankful for under your picture.

A photographer took school pictures in the little white clapboard house in the center of the courtyard, which the three school buildings all backed onto. On photo day a couple of classes got cut short, and boys could buy a comb for a quarter that said "unbreakable" on it. (Believe me, a little elbow grease and that thing snapped like a twig.) Emmet and I had to comb our hair with Score hair grease that smelled like perfumey soap. Your hair got glued together into a solid piece, like a helmet. Score came out of a tube and was bluish-green. If you flicked your finger against the tube, it made a hollow, quivery noise.

The photographer set up his back-drops in one little room. They were gay-looking screens that looked like clouds, or the insides of certain marbles. The photographer always faked one time like he was getting set to pop the flash, just to get you to practice your smile. Then he said a corny line when it was time for you to really smile. You couldn't help smiling then, because he was such a tool.

The photographer was always the same guy all the years that I had been going to school there, and he always said the same thing to me, to make me smile. He made a joke about my head. I might have found that joke super hilarious when I was in first grade, but it had really gotten pretty old over the years. He'd futz around with his camera, and then turn and smile at me.

It's not that your head is big, it's just that the world is so small, he'd say, and laugh like he'd been tickled pink. He had a beard, so when he laughed you saw all these white teeth through the straggly brown hairs, like in a Wolfman horror movie.

My father didn't like pictures, and he thought we all made too much of a fuss about them.

What do I want to see a picture for? he said. I see you every day.

But I'm not always going to look this way.

Thank God for small favors.

On Thursday, February 6, the day Sister French conked out, I had to serve the 6 AM Mass, which was a death day memorial mass day for Saint Paul Miki and his companions, who were Jesuit martyrs in Japan. Catholics celebrate a saint's death day because it was supposed to be great that the day you die is your birthday into eternal life, but I don't know about that.

But St. Miki's story was cool, so you would think that starting off the day with a Mass for him would give me some good luck. Guess again. It was one of the worst days of my life.

Miki could have become a Samurai if he had wanted but became a Christian instead. In 1596, just a few months before he would have been ordained as the first Japanese Catholic priest ever, he was arrested and his ears were cut off as a sign of disgrace. A few weeks later, Miki and two other Jesuits were crucified along with twenty-three other Christians. It sounds like they could make a movie out of that, kind of like a Billy Jack movie, but in the olden days. Miki was only twenty-seven. He was crucified in Nagasaki, where about 450 years later they dropped the big one.

But then officially began the worst day of my life. There was a class discussion about abortion, and we watched a filmstrip called "Is Legalized Killing Wrong?" That gave it away right from the start. Killing was always wrong because it was a sin. And laws were made by people, but only God could tell you what a sin was. We also looked at The Visible Fetus model, this gross little plastic doll stuck inside a plastic stomach. You could see half of the stomach from inside and half of it from outside. It looked like a big gray walnut. We studied what parts of the doll were already fully formed in the second trimester, like the fingers, and about how it already had eyelashes. That stuff.

We were having a discussion about abortion that wasn't a discussion. We had already had The Visible Man and The Visible Woman in there for science class in sixth and seventh grade, and there were the usual jokes and wisecracks about sex. A guy had been invited by Sister Ted to come do a presentation to the class, because he ran the pro-life booth in front of the abortion clinic. He gave a slide show of all these pictures of gross aborted fetuses that looked like Spaghetti-Os.

He started out by reading this long section from the Bible:

> Thou hast protected me from my mother's womb. I will praise thee, for thou art fearfully magnified: wonderful are thy works, and my soul knoweth right well. My bone is not hidden from thee, which thou hast made in secret: and my substance in the lower parts of the earth. Thy eyes did see my imperfect being, and in thy book all shall be written: days shall be formed, and no one in them.

"In order to make it possible for Americans to get an abortion whenever they wanted one," the man then said, leaning down with his hand in the chalk tray of the blackboard, "the bloodthirsty women's movement used the strategy of making the preborn child seem not-human: the baby was always referred to as a 'zygote' or a 'blob of tissue,' a 'fetus,' or a 'product of conception.' If they didn't say the unborn infant was human, they did not have to face (so they thought) the moral consequence of murdering it.

"I am going to show some slides, and they are not pretty. In accordance with the Right to Life movement's guiding principle that every human has the inalienable right to life beginning at fertilization, I have taken the liberty of naming each of these poor little angels.

"This little one was aborted after fourteen weeks gestation. She is named Gabriella."

Eddie Claypool made a gagging noise like he was yakking up a hairball but trying to keep it from leaving his throat. That made me want to laugh, but I held it in.

"Doctors have perfected several methods of eliminating 'non-humans' such as Gabriella. The methods include saline injection, suction, brain suction. This baby, Thomas, was dismembered alive in-utero."

"Yum yum!" Eddie whispered right behind me.

"Abortionists use several methods of disposal including sale of tissue, cremation, or grinding in a garbage disposal. Sometimes they just put the baby in the garbage: this little one, Christina, was found in a trash can behind an abortion clinic."

The man went on for so long that even Eddie Claypool started to get sick to his stomach. When he was done, he collected all his materials and snapped up the movie screen where he had been showing the slides, and left the room without even looking at Sister Ted. He was one weird dude.

After the pro-life man's routine, Sister Ted started off by writing some very definite things she wanted us to learn about abortion on the blackboard. Then she quizzed us to make sure we had learned them. Sister Ted's quiz went like this: (1) When does human life start? Answer: At conception. (2) Why does life begin then? Answer: Because the soul is fully present in the fetus from the moment of conception.

That's not a discussion. A discussion meant you found out what other people thought, and if sometimes they disagreed with you, you found out why, and that was all right, because it was a discussion.

Back in sixth grade the huge abortion thing started with Roe. Vs. Wade. The nuns and Monsignor Bronk went wacko telling us about how bad it was that people were killing babies, that abortion was murder. Monsignor Bronk told us that the cardinal was the first one who got to speak at the Capitol to the senators about it, and that the rabbis and ministers all had to make another appointment, so that at least Catholics were pretty important when it came to abortion. Everybody was getting mad. It was like maybe the Pope should have told people to use rubbers, instead of having abortions, but he was scared to, because the Pope didn't particularly like rubbers, either.

Why do the nuns care so much about abortion? They don't even want to have any babies. They just want everybody else to have babies who will have to grow up and go to Catholic schools.

But what's a soul? It's true that you can't just put your soul in a box, and look in at it every time you need to know whether it's real or not. Here are some excellent questions about the soul:

1)   Did cavemen have souls?
2)   If you go into a coma, does your soul also go into one?
3)   Do you have to teach yourself what your soul is?
4)   Isn't my soul what I want it to be?
5)   If you tell me you don't have a soul, don't I have to believe you? Aren't you the one who's the authority on that?

These are the kinds of questions I wanted to ask Sister Ted, but I was afraid they would get shoved back down into my pie-hole as fast as a shot. Sister Ted already thought I was a smart-mouth. Peter always had great arguments about abortion, but he was afraid to use them in front of Sister Ted.

"Why are you afraid? Your parents would stick up for you. Your aunt would sue everybody if they tried to kick you out."

"I know that," Peter said. "I'm just afraid Sister Ted will pull my hair." Sister Ted was known for sometimes pulling hair, which was illegal, but nobody told on her because they were afraid the next time she pulled their hair, she'd rip up the entire scalp and their brains would be hanging down in mid-air like a shoelace falling out of the package.

Eddie Claypool said, "My ma says she's for abortion."

"Bull."

"She is. After birth and up until the fetus moves out of the house." Eddie Claypool giggled like a moe.

"I don't know what I think," I said. "I don't like killing a baby, but I hate to be on Sister Ted's side."

"But it's the woman's body," Peter said. "It's *inside* her. It's like me telling you that from now on, I'll make all the decisions about your liver."

"No it isn't," I said. I didn't really get it, but I was willing to let Peter tell me how it really was. Sometimes you do that if you've got a really good friend.

✿   ✿   ✿

Sister Ted was a total pain in the A. She never said anything she hadn't thought out completely, so she was hard to trip up. Also, she never leaves any room for me to talk about one of her ideas.

After the filmstrip and soul quiz, we had social studies, where we were studying the 1940s in American politics. We split up into different groups. Each group had to act like they were running the 1948 presidential campaign for a different candidate. My group had bad luck and pulled a loser's name—Henry Wallace. He ran against Truman, which was like running against God.

Not only did Henry Wallace lose big time, but he was a socialist and didn't hate the Russians as much as everybody else in the world, which everybody thinks is exactly the same thing as being a communist, but it isn't, as I found out. Communists are always bad. Some socialists are okay.

My group was mostly cool people. They all did nothing, but you couldn't yell at them, because they were cool, and only cool people could make you feel cool for reading stuff that they didn't want to read. So I did all of the reading, because the cool people said I was the man, I was the one who could win us the election. But all they really wanted was for me to get them a good grade.

From the very first, the people in my class (including my teammates) hated Henry Wallace, because they thought he was actually George Wallace, the Southerner, who wouldn't let black kids go to his state's college. He just stood in front of the door like a big redneck, hating black people.

"Nope," George Wallace had said. "Y'all can*not* come on in."

Old Henry Wallace had some pretty good ideas, which goes to show you can lose big time, but still not be a big-time loser. He knew his party was unpopular, but he believed in his ideas, and he loved America, too. What's so wrong with that? He was vice president, but FDR dumped him in 1944 because FDR thought he was whacked, so Wallace formed the Progressive Party. The Progressives wanted all the countries in the world to give up their weapons, and they wanted to give the vote to eighteen year olds, and create a Department of Culture and a food stamp program, all ideas that were way ahead of their time. But poor old Henry only got two percent of the popular vote.

Politics is about power, according to my father. He won't even vote anymore because of Nixon. But he does say that even though Nixon was a creep and a crumb, he was smart and he understood power. When he first ran for senator in California, and his opponent was a woman, old Tricky Dick printed up information about the woman on pink paper just to make her seem weak. And he won, too.

When my father comes up with a good one like that, it seems like he makes it up, but I repeat it to other people anyhow, to sound like a know-it-all.

❁ ❁ ❁

The debate ended up a mess, but I gave a pretty good speech on spheres of influence, which was Henry Wallace's big deal about how it was okay that Russia was controlling half the world, as long as America was controlling the other half. I was on a roll until my so-called friend Fitz Patrick, who was being Truman, interrupted me. Ray Lasher was also on the Truman team, and I saw him and Fitz huddled together shuffling their papers together. Then Fitz stood up.

"Are you a socialist or a communist, Mr. Wallace, and what's the big dif anyway?"

I started to say that there was a difference, that everyone knows socialists aren't half as bad as communists, but Ray jumped up and shouted "You're nothing but a communist! You want the Soviet Union to take over America."

"No, I don't. I'm trying to answer the question that Fitz—"

"His name is Harry S. Truman," Sister Ted said proudly.

Fitz said, "Yes, you do want Russia to take over America."

"Yeah!" somebody else on his team said.

"U-S-A, U-S-A!" Fitz yelled.

Everybody in the class starting going "YEAH, YEAH!"

"At least Henry Wallace wasn't from stupid old Missouri!" It was my last shot, but nobody even heard me. We voted afterward and Truman creamed me. I got three votes and, yes, I voted for myself. When the bell rang my face was pretty red, because I was sort of sad for myself for looking like a big cry baby with a red face. But also I was a little sad for Henry Wallace, who wasn't a commie at all, just different. Then Sister Ted saw me walking to my next class, with this tough look on my face I only get if I really *am* afraid I might cry a little.

I usually hope my glasses will cover it up, if a couple of tears do fall out. The last time I actually cried was last Christmas, watching this after school TV special called "JT," about this little black boy in the ghetto, who was so poor he had to eat soup crackers crumbled up in a bowl of milk for his breakfast. He found a little black-and-white kitten in an abandoned building and built a little house for it in a thrown-away stove that was just lying around there, but some guys from a gang found the kitten, who he had named Bones, and they killed it. JT wore a cap that had earflaps you could fold up and snap into place, and he carried a transistor radio up there that he had stolen out of somebody's car.

I also cried at *Gigot* where Jackie Gleason was a mute, and got in trouble with these A-holes and couldn't explain that he didn't do it. That was a long time ago, so I forget what they actually were saying he did. Or maybe he was in love with a girl and couldn't tell her about it. It was something like that.

In the hallway Sister Ted says, out of the blue, since I was not talking and had stayed in line and everything, "Don't you look at me that way, Digby Shaw! You can just wipe that look right off your face RIGHT NOW!"

Then I made the mistake of showing her just how mad I really was by talking back.

"What look? I'm not looking at you at all," I said.

That just drives her wacko, to be told that any of her students weren't looking at her moronic face every second of every day. I think she was also touchy because Sister French, who was her buddy, had gone nutso before lunch, which I'll get to soon. Sister Ted pulled me out of line by my arm and yelled at me about giving her lip, and how I was a sore loser. I wanted to ask her if she thought it was fair that Fitz had called me a commie, but I couldn't, because then I would have started crying for sure. Everybody was looking at me, and the line had practically stopped moving.

There was one girl named Cissy Snodgrass in Sister French's homeroom who bugged her all the time. She played the Virgin Mary for a couple of years in the Passion Play, and she had the only known crush on Solomon "Flutterbug" Mars in the history of St. Tabasco Elementary School.

It started when at one point during math class that day, Sister French had told Cissy to get up and to stand by the side of her desk.

"And get your hair out of your face," Sister French snapped.

"It's my hair, said Cissy. She did get up from her desk, but she kept her face turned to the side, so that the girl sitting in back of her, Marge Thurston, could see that Cissy Snodgrass was smiling to beat the band.

Sister French wore her own hair in little tight black rows of curls. You could just see the edges of them, sticking out from under her cap like little logs. All the nuns wore caps, like train conductors. Sister French also had all the usual wet palms and sweaty smells of nuns.

"I *know* it's your hair, but I still want you to get it out of your face," Sister French told Cissy. Cissy raised her right hand really slowly and pushed back her long, light-brown hair.

Cissy was not really pretty, but she had nice hair. Every day she came to school and displayed her hair in homeroom. She arranged it on her shoulders, and kept tossing her head back and forth until each hair looked like it was ready to ramble. Then she just sat there as if she were waiting for people to come up and genuflect in front of her.

Most of the time, Sister French just sat at her desk in the front of the room. Any time she had to talk to Cissy, though, she scooted her chair back a couple of inches and set both her feet on the floor, like maybe she was going to make a break for it. Sister French wore black lace-up shoes that looked like they were made out of iron. She gripped the edge of her desk with both hands.

Cissy Snodgrass sat down again, and as soon as she was sitting, she turned her head right around to whisper something to Marge. Marge also talked too much in class, but she wasn't as bad as Cissy. Marge was just stupid, like a rock. Then Cissy whipped her head around fast, so that her hair splayed out again all over her face.

"Go to the principal's office *now*," Sister French shouted. Cissy picked up her bookbag, even though you were supposed to ask if you should take your books with you if you got sent to the principal's office. Then Cissy walked right up next to Sister French's desk, and she leaned over so that their faces were almost touching.

"Am I standing up tall now?" she asked Sister French. Sister French just looked at her, and then she went back to staring straight ahead to where Cissy Snodgrass's desk was, as if Cissy were still standing next to it. Cissy reached out and took one of the little log-curls that was peeping out of Sister French's cap, and she pulled on it hard, just once. In back of me, Eddie Claypool gasped out loud. Even he had never touched a nun. Then Cissy walked right back to her desk, dropped her bookbag beside it, and sat back down again.

Sister French was still staring at Cissy's desk. It was a very nervous time because she was looking at it for too long. Then a couple of kids tried to ask her some questions, about what notebook to open up. Then some other kids raised their hands, and just stared at each other's hands for a while. Then nobody raised their hands any more, and everybody started talking out loud.

"Sister!"

"Sister French!"

Half the people ignored her altogether and were chattering together like it was right before the bell, when the rule about being quiet gets a little loose, because everyone, even the teacher, is looking up at the clock.

"Sister French, do we have—"

"Is there homework in math, Sister?"

But Sister French wasn't paying any attention to them. If she had been a magnifying glass, and Cissy Snodgrass had been an ant, smoke would have been coming out from between Cissy's fried antenna right about then. Then Sister French started sobbing. She wasn't really crying, because there weren't tears rolling down her cheeks, but she was making a sound like she was humming and hiccupping at the same time. Bartos Cuscusmontrous, who sat in front of Cissy Snodgrass, turned around and looked at her.

"Now luke what you deed."

"*I* didn't do anything," Cissy replied. She didn't even look at him but continued her smiling visit with Marge Thurston.

"Then why ees she cryng?"

"Cissy didn't *do* anything," Marge Thurston shot back at Bartos.

"Maybe she's just a big baby," Cissy Snodgrass said. She screeched and giggled. Slim said that that seemed to wake up Sister French, and she stood straight up behind her desk. Now her face *was* wet. The whites of her eyes looked really red, like little radishes. Sister French kept her hands on her desk as she stood up, and she just stood there and cried and cried and cried.

Pretty soon somebody went down and got Sister Skeletona. She came into the classroom and put her arm around Sister French and stood her up and walked her over to the door.

"Read quietly at your desk," Sister Skeletona said. "I'll be back to deal with you later," but nobody read anything. We all just whispered about what might happen next.

Love Story

One time I went to see the movie *Love Story* with my father. We wanted to see *Billy Jack*, but it was sold out. *Love Story* was the only other movie playing, and let me tell you, it is not the greatest movie to see with your father.

It was pretty mushy, even if there were some good hockey fights in it. The guy falls in love with a tough girl who curses a lot. He's not Catholic, but she is, so his parents don't want them to get married. Well, we're Catholic, so whose side are we supposed to be on? Catholics are always getting dicked. Just like the girl in *Love Story*. Because she was Catholic, it was a big deal that she constantly said the F-word. Maybe that's why she had to be the one who died.

When she was first dating the guy, he left a tie on the door as a signal to his roommate that he was strapping her, and that meant that the roommate should just cruise on to somewhere else to sleep, but they never told you where he went. It was supposed to be a big deal about her even *wanting* to be strapped.

Everybody who isn't Catholic expected you to want to be weaker than you were, and to always be dying to do everything you're not supposed to. But the nuns and priests want you to be stronger than you are. Still, it must be pretty boring to be a nun or a priest, which is probably why they have to pull a couple of fast ones every once in a while, just to stay in the practice of being like normal people.

My father must have thought that we wandered into the wrong movie by mistake, since this one got pretty heavy into the making out. Then they try to have a baby, but she gets really sick instead and goes in the hospital, and in the end she's lying in the hospital bed, and she asks her husband to climb into the bed right next to her. Then at the very end she dies, and the guy is sad, but he hugs his father, who he always thought he hated before that. More of the big dif about being happy or being sad. What goes around comes around, my ma says. She also says, I might have been born at night, but not last night.

During the whole movie my father was making noises in his seat next to me, like he was starting to say something, and then stopping himself.

"Hmpphh hmmm," he said, into his hand.

"What?"

When there was any dirty stuff at all, my father coughed a lot, but I could still hear the cussing pretty clearly. Since he smokes, it could have just been normal coughing. He made us bolt as soon as the credits started to roll. Usually I like to wait for the lights to come on, so I can spot the couples who've been making out, who are always still slumped down in their seats.

Right here in my scrapbook is my first grade class photo, where my picture is right next to the picture of the first girl I ever had a dirty dream about. Her name was Stephanie Scotch, but nobody in her family was Scottish. I don't know where she is now. She always wore turtlenecks, with a locket necklace that got caught in the collar.

There was nothing *really* dirty about the dream. We started going into a big fluffy circular cloud that looked like a cake pan, but then I realized our clothes were about to disappear off our bodies. Nobody knows about that dream. It seems weird to see it written down here right in front of me. It makes it feel like it's not still secret. When I woke up, all I was really thinking about was eating a big piece of angel food cake. Sometimes I lie awake and wish that the daydream I always have would drop me off in first grade every once in a while, so I could have that dream again. It was something. Made me feel like I had a fishbowl in my pants.

When I remember being happy, I can see the space I was in and even that, in the memory, seems pretty happy. But when I'm sad, all I remember is the time it takes to feel happy again. It's like when you get a splinter. You pull at it and tug at it, and it finally disappears or it falls out, but you keep going back to the spot to rub it. You're remembering how bad it felt. But your skin is remembering it like it was happy.

Sometimes, when I was playing baseball when I was little, I felt like I'd never been so happy in my life. I just stood out there in right field, which was the worst position, and barely better than not playing at all. I'd be chewing this one disgusting leather string on my glove that had come untied a long time before and that I'd never retied. I chewed on the string every summer because I never had anything else to do out in right field. I wasn't even that hungry. I'd bring up my glove like I was blocking the sun out of my eyes, and then I'd put the string on my tongue and chow down.

There was a lot of waiting in right field. There was almost no chance a ball would be hit to me unless there was a lefty at the plate or somebody swung too late. What would I do if it happened? I'd say to myself, No out, play's at first if it's on the ground or throw to the cut-off if it's in the air.

Then there was the swing, and my legs jerked forward toward the plate no matter what happened. Then it would be a strike, and I had moved for nothing, or it was a routine grounder to the infield, and I'd run to be backup, but of course I never got there in time.

And all winter that little piece of leather had hardened like a piece of plastic.

That's it, I'd say to myself in the spring when I saw it again. Grow up. It's too disgusting to chew on anymore. Buy gum if you have to chew. But by the beginning of July, hootie-hoo! It was back and softer than cotton. It was so soft it started to dissolve in my mouth. It didn't taste like food, but it still didn't taste that bad. I could have stood there until doomsday as long as nothing happened. And nothing kept happening. The sun was so slow and hot it was barely moving. People in the stands were frozen in place like dolls. Even the infield and the batter seemed like they were in another game that I was watching through a telescope.

Then CRACK, somebody lined one down the first-base line (*Fair ball!*) I was slow at first and slower once I picked up speed. The coach would yell at me before I even reached the ball, PICK UP YOUR KNEES! And the ball got past me, and the guy got to second instead of it just being a routine single, unless my throw in was wild and curved, in which case he may have ended up on third.

But then I would just trudge back to my trampled place in the grass and start up chewing again, and everything quieted down, and I was happy.

I had called up Maxine on the phone a couple of nights before and read stuff out loud to her. Let me tell you right out, Maxine wasn't the smartest girl in our school. She was in the lowest section, and I knew that part of the reason she even liked me at all was she thought I was a brain. But I'm an idiot compared to Darwin Mars, and a complete mongoloid next to Peter Kiernan.

Mrs. Myna had been giving me funny looks when I kept showing up at their front door after dinner. She knew that I knew that Jake had basketball practice every day (except Mondays after games), so I must have been there for something else. So I got paranoid and I stopped going over every day after school. Still, I thought about Maxine like crazy. I'd go home after school and moon around the window looking toward the Myna's house. So I started the phone calls.

If anybody but Maxine answered, I would ask for Jake. If Maxine answered, I'd start making something up. It was just her voice, but that was something. When you were in love with somebody and you couldn't be with her, you got mad all the time if other people were around you, but at the same time it was too sad to be alone, so you were just miserable, period. That was hairy.

The first time we talked on the phone I was looking out my parents' bedroom window, and I could just see the corner of her house through a bunch of trees. We talked about school. It wasn't really interesting. There were long pauses like she was doing something else. Then she asked me to read something to her out loud over the phone.

"What do you mean?" I asked nervously. I said before that Maxine wasn't a rocket scientist. Sometimes, when I thought she meant something more than what I understood her to mean, she actually meant something less. Like once, she had asked me if I knew anything about tennis shots. I said Yeah, a little. Then Maxine said, I have to get a tennis shot tomorrow, and I hate shots. I stepped on a nail, and now it's turning purple, so I have to get the shot.

"I want you to read me something out loud over the phone. Something you wrote," she said.

Well, I couldn't do that because I didn't have anything prepared. I told her I'd get a book. I set the phone down and ran down to the bookcase in the rec room, and pulled down the first book that caught my eye, which happened to be a book of Herblock cartoons of my father's. It wasn't the something you could really read aloud over the phone, even if the cartoons were funny, especially the ones that have this big tough-guy character who was supposed to be the A-Bomb.

I had to get back to the phone fast, so I just went with it. I ended up describing the pictures to Maxine over the phone, and then reading the captions. She would ask me to go back and describe the picture again pretty often, and then I would have to read the caption again. It got pretty confusing, but even if it was embarrassing, we got a couple of good laughs out of it. And somehow or another it was flirty, too.

That was a good call, because it was just as easy to have a bad one, when you were already in some kind of messy situation in the house. Your ma was shooting you looks that pulled your hair, and your father was stomping around upstairs slamming the bathroom door. Molly was crying, Emmet was under the table drawing with magic markers, and Maud came out of her room every five seconds to say, I have to make a call NOW, Digby! Ma! Ma! He's hogging the phone, Ma!

So the phone could go either way.

That night, though, I was ready. I had found a book of Molly's called *Maxine and Her Paper Bags*, about this little girl who had a million old grocery bags that she kept under the bed and played with. It was not great, but girls are suckers for baby stuff, and Maxine dug it. When I was done reading it, she told me to come over, but to come to the basement door. When I got there, Maxine was waiting downstairs. She took me by the hand without saying anything. We went into Jake's room, turned off the light, lay on his bed, and made out like crazy. Ricky Seerser the retard came into the room at one point, but Maxine just pushed him back outside, locked the door, and jumped back on top of me.

The air outside was cold. I cruised by the Myna's and acted like I was looking for Jake when Maxine answered the door. And then she acted like it didn't matter that I was just waiting and talking to her.

While I stood at their door, Ricky Seerser had been pulling his wagon around the block in front of his house, right there across the street from the Mynas. After I went in, he immediately came up to the front door. When Maxine didn't answer, he went around to the back door and just trucked on inside, saying Maxine! a couple of times. He wanted to play.

One thing about the Mynas, they always made Ricky feel at home. He could come and go whenever he wanted. One of the Mynas always took him home when his mother rang the big bell by their kitchen door. Mrs. Myna fed him all the time, and Mr. Myna shook hands with him any time he saw him, because Ricky Seerser loved to shake hands. All the Myna boys roughhoused with him, fake-tackling him and throwing his balls near him for him to go pick up, like he was a dog. That also made him happy like crazy. Maxine hugged him whenever the bell rang and he had to leave, and he was so happy to be hugged by her that he knew how to say her name. It was the only name he knew how to say, in the whole world.

I don't know exactly what Ricky Seerser does during the day, but I do know that he gets on a schoolbus and goes to a special retard school. He carries three balls with him at all times wherever he goes: a tennis ball, a football, and a kickball.

Ricky hit adolescence early. That's what Fitz says, who is just starting to get an Adam's Apple himself. (Fitz's half-sister Bonnie once cornered me in their rec room right on the steps. She had strawberry lip-smacker on and she breathed all over my lips. I got such an immediate ten-hut I almost passed out, but more on her later.)

Ricky Seerser's face is almost a rectangle. His chin is a horizontal straight line like Dudley Dooright from the *Rocky and Bullwinkle Show*. Ricky looks like he needs a shave all the time, even though he's only a year older than me. I've never even shaved once. I do have some hair under my arms. If you look really hard you can see it, but why would you? Ricky's hair is black and wavy and it's always brushed to the right side in a little part.

He wears regular clothes that always look brand new. The pants have deep, sharp creases in them, sharp like there's a hacksaw blade underneath them. His shirts always have that little wrinkle right in the middle of the back, from the factory, which goes away as soon as most guys wear the shirt once.

Ricky Seerser doesn't wear glasses, but when I see him looking at something, sometimes I think he needs them. He stares for a long time, and then squint his eyes at whatever he's looking at, even if it's just his bicycle or his kickball, things he sees every day.

He likes to watch people do stuff, and he gets excited like a little baby when he sees something being done that is cool to him, like smashing or anything noisy, or something that goes back and forth a lot, like having a catch. But he would never do anything by himself. He can't. If there were no one taking care of him, he would stand in the same spot and bounce his balls until he starved to death and fell over right there like an old tree.

Since he lives right behind me, there's not a big dif between where he lives and where I live. Sometimes I think it could have been me that could have been him. I wish it could have been him that had all the trouble I had in the past six months, but I know it's not that simple, to trade places like that just because you're neighbors. Still, it's hard to figure out how a guy who lives fifty feet from me every minute of my life could live a zillion miles away in his mind, in what he's like inside.

He's not even retarded really. He's brain-damaged. He can't learn at all; he can just imitate easy stuff. I think his mother gave birth to him really early, so when he came out he wasn't ready, and his brain didn't get enough air. Like taking bread out of the oven before it's risen, and it looks gooey and smells bad, even if you could still eat it, if you were starving.

Ricky goes wild sometimes when he knows he's getting hurt or when he's mad or just doesn't know what to do. When he goes wild he's the strongest person in the whole neighborhood by far, stronger than Jake or even Jake's brother Jeff, who can lift up the wheel of a Volkswagen all by himself. He's probably even stronger than most fathers. When Ricky Seerser grabs you by the shoulder, you feel like you're going to split right down the middle like a piece of paper.

We went outside with Ricky into that cold dark night, and he got his wagon. We hadn't been doing anything in the house. I had sat in an armchair, and Maxine had been lying on the couch, and we threw around a pillow for a while. Maxine was wearing her big old orange down coat, so she was really puffed out, but very warm. I was wearing an old baseball jacket like I was Joe Cool, but I was freezing to death and having to act like I wasn't. In other words, I was a cold asshole.

Ricky was wearing a belted winter coat, a hat like an old man's with a red feather in it, gloves, and hard shoes. He was dressed like a little German prince going to the palace. You see, his mother dresses him. Maxine and I were laughing, because it was a little ridiculous to be playing with a retarded guy in the middle of a school night at our ages, more than halfway through the eighth grade.

We got in his wagon anyway, and Ricky started pulling us. I already said he is strong as an ox, and likes doing hard stuff. After all, he's mental. Maxine was in front, so I got in the back. She didn't even turn around all the way. "Put your arms around me, so you won't fall off," she said over her shoulder, like she was telling me to have a nice day. It was a good idea, though, because I barely fit back there, and I almost did fall off when Ricky gave the first jerk on the handle to get us going.

I put my arms around her chest, but outside her damn puffy coat. Then, the miracle happened. She grabbed my hands in hers and pulled them apart, and then she brought them down to waist-level and up under the front of the coat, and over her chest. Instantly I turned ragingly horny, like a horned toad who comes up out of a dark pond in the middle of a full moon, and who is covered with bumps because he is so ready to do it.

We clunked along the sidewalk. It was so perfect I was almost sick. My hands started out very carefully, just holding on to her boobs, which was definitely what they were, boobs made out of flesh, not just a big bra. I would have known if it was just a bra I was feeling, because I had gone to the bra base before. It was not really a base at all. It was more like getting trapped between the bases in a hotbox, and you have to decide whether to get back to first and just be happy with doing some more kissing, or whether to take the chance of getting totally busted, by digging your fingers underneath the bra.

You might say I was an expert on running that hotbox, because I have given many deadly bra-snappers. It was easy to do if the girl had never gotten a snapper from you before. You just acted like you were patting her back. She thought you were being friendly, so then you slipped your horny forefinger over and under the snap in the middle of her back, connected your thumb to your finger, and pulled back like you were Robin Hood. Wham!

I'm an expert on other perverted stuff, too. For example, to be able to see through a skirt, the sun had to be in front of the girl. Even then you just saw her legs, and personally I could care less about legs. What's the big deal if a girl had great legs and a face like a donkey? No thanks. Maxine had big legs, but she also had a pretty face, and a few other goodies. It was really the thought that you were looking at a girl's legs, and she didn't even know it, that was so great. Sometimes you saw the little out-line of her underpants standing out against the material of the skirt. Underneath that is the vagina, which apparently has at least two holes, a pee hole and a plop hole. But I've also heard about a third hole, and there's also some type of a slit. So it's going to be pretty busy down there.

What I was feeling in my hands, riding in Ricky Seerser's wagon, was not cotton padding. I just about broke my fingers spreading them as wide as they could go, and I rested my head on Maxine's neck and smelled her great hair smell. It could have smelled like crap, and I would have still inhaled it like it was oxygen and I hadn't breathed in a year. Maxine was leaning back into me, and she kept her hands on top of my hands, like she was afraid I'd let go if she didn't keep them in place.

Like I would have let go. In a million years I might have. Maxine should have been worrying about me never letting go, since I was plan-ning on becoming attached to her. She was going to have to carry me piggy back into her house, and then explain to her parents what she was doing playing chicken fights with my mitts filled with her tits, my face still buried in her hair, as if we were some sort of weird horny Siamese twins, like the ones in the *Guinness Book of World Records*.

So we just rode along, two perverts in a metal wagon. It had been freezing cold when we started out, but now I was getting hot. I looked ahead through Maxine's hair, at Ricky pulling us around and around the same block, across the same four corners. He always made a little extra grunting noise on the turn. There were clouds of steam coming out of his mouth and flying back over his shoulder like a ghost scarf.

I wondered what Ricky was thinking about, or if he was even think-ing. He must have been thinking about something, because they say that everybody's thinking all the time, even when they're asleep. I figured Ricky wasn't thinking about me at all. Even though he lived right behind me, and I played with him every once in a while, like everybody else, and always said his name when I saw him, he had never said *my* name. Maybe he was thinking about Maxine, since she hugged him, and he was always over at the Mynas' house. I wondered if he ever thought about Maxine's breasts, if he even knew what a breast was and if he'd ever seen one. Maybe he thought boobs were just big shirts that girls wore.

He certainly wasn't thinking that it was in his wagon, of all the places in the world, that I became the happiest goof on the planet.

After a while, Ricky started huffing and puffing from all the exercise.

After about fifteen minutes of that, we tried to stop him, but he got really excited and was about to throw a fit, so we just let him keep going. I was smoothing my hands around Maxine's body in the same wide circles, trying to be gentle like I was petting an animal who might run away if I got any rougher. At one point one of her hands came back without a mitten on it, and she ran it through my hair and said "Mmmmm," like she was just waking up.

Right after I thought about whether Ricky could think or not, I thought about Maxine being pregnant. I was too happy and giddy to think about it for very long, but it flashed through my mind, her big stomach and these little feet kicking inside her, like the baby was trying to get out of a paper bag. Then I was back in the wagon, in heaven, with my arms around her. I thought of me and her getting married, and her pregnant with a little miniature version of me, and all our friends coming over to see the baby.

There was a problem, though, which was this: Maxine was in a clique of cool girls at school, and even though she was not the leader of the clique, it was a bunch of popular pretty girls. They were not really into the science dorks who would drop everything for a chance to snarf up a Big Wheel.

The leaders of the clique were Belinda Wellman, Sue Condor, Tessa Trueblood (who was small but had really hard breasts, according to George Gack, but don't ask me how he knew it), and Sandy Villa, who Fitz Patrick said he had laid when he was in first grade. The Cool Clique did everything together. They all started on the eighth-grade basketball team. They had sleepovers together that were legendary, because sometimes they invited guys over and played Spin The Bottle, and one time Fitz said that Sandy Villa took off her underpants, but she kept on her pajama bottoms, so I don't really get what's the big deal.

The clique always had one not-cool girl who they were trying to recruit by getting her to wear makeup and seeing if they could get her a guy. That used to be Maxine, but now she wore eye shadow almost every day and was working her way through the eighth-grade boys like she was flipping through a stack of 45s looking for a copy of "Why Can't We Be Friends?" They hadn't replaced her yet with a new not-cool girl.

So my daydream got sad, with Maxine sitting there on the sofa with this baby looking up at her like a puppy, and all her girlfriends chucking the little guy under the chin, and me sitting across the room sweating into my armchair, making stupid comments that made the cool girls roll their eyes and pull up one side of their mouth like I was a sourball they were about to loog out into the grass. I tried to switch it back to the regular daydream about waking up again in the second grade but I couldn't; the baby wouldn't disappear; he just sat there and laughed and spat at me like he was a little fountain.

Eddie Claypool
the Pope

Eddie Claypool the Pope sat behind me in social studies and whispered about Veronica Lodge and the things he would do to her boobs if he ever got his hands on them. That's Veronica from the *Archie* comic books. She was rich and a snob but hot as hell. Archie loved her, but he was poor and had gross freckles (so did Eddie), so Veronica never took him seriously.

Eddie Claypool moaned and twisted in his seat when he talked about Veronica. He sat inside his desk and moved it all the way across the floor just by twisting it and pulling it forward with his feet. He breathed onto my neck like it was Veronica's belly button. Oh Ronnie! Oww-wow ruff!

A lot of the same rules applied to the *Archie* girls that also applied to *Gilligan's Island*, where if you were smart you went for Marianne, instead of Ginger, because there was less competition. Veronica was definitely a little prettier than Betty, and much richer, but if you looked closely you saw they both had exactly the same rack. The cartoonist must have been bored with drawing boobs, because all the girls had exactly the same ones, except for Jughead's girlfriend, who was even more disgusting than he was, and flat as splat. But the stupidest possible thing would have been to have the hots for Midge, Moose's girlfriend, because Moose might smoosh you if you weren't careful. He was constantly smooshing Archie just for being on the same street as her.

Eddie Claypool had a way of looking at you with his head rolled back a little on his neck, so that he watched you on a slant. You had to be careful, because you'd think he was looking up at the ceiling, but if you went to give him a little punch, he'd grab your arm quick as a whip by the wrist, and fake-knee you in the nads. He was skinny, but not because he didn't eat. Eddie ate all the time. He brought in Scooter Pies and Mounds bars, and even cashew nuts, and ate them right at his desk like it was snack time.

Way after lunch, everyone would be working at their desks, and I'd hear this crinkly noise, and turn around. Good old Eddie Claypool would be unwrapping a Scooter Pie he was holding between his knees under his desk. He'd unwrap it blind, because he'd be looking straight at me and grinning to beat the band.

Ain't I slick? he whispered across the aisle.

Eddie Claypool *was* slick. His dad worked as a bagger at the local Grand Union, which you wouldn't think was much, but Eddie said his dad made eighteen dollars an hour, because he was in the Grand Union union. His mother was an old-people nurse, and Eddie said that one time an old man tried to leave her all his money, which was a half a million bucks, but the old dude's relatives wouldn't let her have it.

Eddie Claypool wrote a haiku once called "The Sun":

> I am yellow
> Your yellow fellow
>
> I light the sky
> And never die
>
> I don't shine at night
> Cause I'm out of sight!

It's completely wrong. Even Bartos Cuscusmontrous, who was some kind of Spic, wrote a better one than that:

> My friend,
> my very good friend,
> I want you to come over
> to learn some new tricks,

Although we certainly made fun of him for that, since it was completely wrong in the number of lines and syllables, and syllables were the whole point of writing haikus in the first place. You don't have to be a robot to remember 5-7-5.

At the end of fourth grade, I found out I was going to be in a different homeroom than Eddie Claypool for fifth grade. In my autograph book he wrote *You trader* in red pen, with blood dripping from the letters, then below that he wrote *see you sucker*, and below that he wrote *you may be fat but your beer is good tears tears boohoo*.

Eddie Claypool also taught me how to say "fuck" in fourth grade. We both thought it was the funniest word in the whole world. We didn't care what it meant but it felt hilarious to say it, like screaming at the top of your lungs, except you didn't have to scream at all. Then Eddie's father began constantly threatening that he was going to transfer him to a public school. It was when we had a spelling test that he taught me it. Eddie got a 37 percent, by far the lowest mark. There was red ballpoint pen slashed all over it, like Mrs. Sumbutts had spazzed out when she was marking it. He looked over on my desk. I had got a 92 percent - V. Good.

"Fuck!" Eddie Claypool gasped.

"Fuck it," I whispered back. Since I used it right, he and I were better friends. And then in eighth grade, Eddie Claypool played the Pope in the Elizabeth Ann Seton Canonization play.

Peter and I were going to ruin Sister Ted's Seton play, which was the latest thing she was doing to bore the entire eighth grade back into the Stone Age. It was to be a play about the new Saint's life. Part of the biggest deal the nuns were making about Elizabeth Ann Seton was that she was the first native-born saint, but what they don't tell you right away about her is that she wasn't even born Catholic! She converted from being a Protestant.

We asked Eddie Claypool's older brother Oscar to help us, because he loved musicals and was a good actor. Oscar had either run away from home or was kicked out of the house, depending on who you asked. Eddie's father thought Oscar was living with their mother. They had just gotten a divorce. It was a totally screwed-up family. Oscar was living on the banks of Sligo Creek so he could still be in the musicals at his high school. Mr. Claypool didn't want him to be in musicals anymore. Oscar was nice but a little queer. He wanted to be an actor and he was always racing around with a scarf around his neck talking about rehearsals. He was in *Harvey* last year when he was a freshman in high school, and I went with Eddie to see it. It was stupid. The guy who Oscar played kept saying that he could see this big white rabbit, but that was BS because there was no rabbit. Eddie and I kept waiting for the rabbit to show, but it was no deal. That's bull. Now, if they had just brought on out the big bunny, even if it was just some guy in a bunny suit, that would have been different. That might have been something to see.

We met one night after dinner at the Kiernans' house. Oscar made us do a bunch of gay stretching exercises, and then we had to play the trust game, where I stood in front of Peter and just let myself fall backward, and Peter caught me, and then we switched places.

"These are great, Oscar, but we don't really need acting lessons," I panted after an exercise where I had to be a lawnmower and Peter was a leaf blowing around the lawn and I had to try to catch him and cut him.

"I thought you said you needed help with a play you were in," Oscar frowned. He was sitting with his legs all folded up in his lap watching us with this serious look on his face and his palms flat on the ground.

"No, no," Peter said. "You see, the eighth grade is doing this lousy Mother Seton play, because she's going to be a saint, and we want to ruin it. That's why we need your help."

"Oh." Oscar looked sad. "Well, just screw up your lines or mutter. There's a million ways to screw up a play."

"Yeah, but we want to do it right. We want to take over the play and make it mean what we want it to mean."

"What do you want it to mean?"

"We just hate Elizabeth Ann Seton," I said. I was confused myself now. "We're sick of being told what to do and having no freedom!"

Oscar gathered up his stuff and tied his scarf around his neck. "You're in a parochial school," he huffed. "What do you think it's going to be like?"

After Oscar left, all that we could decide about the sabotage was that it would have to be near the end of the play. I convinced Peter that we had to let Sister Ted get a lot of her stupid Seton action over with before we ruined it, because I was afraid of getting expelled so near to graduation. Eddie Claypool was going to rip off his Pope's vest. I would do a Fat Albert laugh. Peter was running lights, so he figured that he could get the spotlight onto Eddie.

The Mother Seton Play was being created, written, directed, staged, and produced by Sister Ted. Elizabeth Ann Seton. was canonized in December of last year, and Sister Ted was acting like she herself was next to be canonized, as soon as people saw her play. Four different girls played the part of Seton, one for when she was a girl and one for when she got older, and a different pair on each of the two performance nights.

Sister Ted's Seton play was dumb. It started out with these four Americans wandering around calling out statistics from our social studies textbook about the USA. Then Saint Seton-head and her family stumbled off a steamship and started settling everywhere.

Later, the Pope showed up, too. Like I said, my friend Eddie Claypool was playing him. Eddie was the only guy in our class who still had a crew-cut, and his ears were always red, like they had just been slapped. His freckles were all over his face and got lighter or darker, depending on whether he had been to the bathroom lately. And he smiled almost all the time, even when he was sad or scared. There was always a little smidge of a grin on his face, so you could see his teeth. When he smiled his eyelids wrinkled and the skin on his temple folded up.

I'm not very good at remembering jokes. I can usually only remember the last one I heard. Eddie Claypool, who sometimes forgets how to spell his own *name*, can remember every joke he's ever heard, who told it to him, and if there are any other jokes like it. Go figure. Bartos Cuscusmontrous was the First American in the play, which was ridiculous because he had the thickest Spanish accent you ever heard. He was the only one in the whole eighth grade you could hear when we said the Pledge of Allegiance in class, because he loved America so much.

"I plahdge aah-eegence do da fag, Bartos sang out.

One time, Sister Ted said, "Bartos is a living example of the melting pot." Bartos grinned like he had just cut a windjammer.

Eddie Claypool said, "Bartos is a living example of a Fat Crap," and got up and went down to the principal's office without even being asked.

One Friday, Eddie and I were having a little fun during rehearsal for the Seton Play. We were sitting in the audience watching the Elizabeths rehearsing their lines. We rolled up our programs into telescopes and looked through them at the girls on stage. We were acting like that made their dresses see-through, and we could check out their breasts that way. The girls got really nervous, even though they didn't really know what the hey we were doing, but it was like they *felt* us looking at their boobs.

Patty Pam Kiernan got to play the part of Elizabeth Ann Seton, but she was only going to play her on the Thursday night show, in the second half of the play. Another girl played EAS in the early years, and two other girls were going to do the parts on the Friday night. Sister Ted had special extended rehearsals for the saint-girls, after the rest of us had finished.

"All right, Elizabeths One-Through-Four, let's meet back in Room 17 for some extra work," Sister Ted would call out, with her clipboard pressed against her hip. I imagined what her knobby red knees must have looked like underneath her woolen skirt. I'll bet they stuck out like bumpy little Munchkin-heads.

Peter and I were a little worried about how Patty Pam would deal with our disrupting the play, since she was a star. Peter had told me stories of being sat on by her that would make your nose bleed.

The only bad thing about Peter Kiernan was his twin sister, Patty Pam, who was the fattest girl in our school, and who had been in love with me for three years straight now, because she thought I was nice. She wore a charm bracelet that was practically buried by her arm fat. Sometimes little heart charms popped out of the folds in her arm, but then she would crook her elbow again, and her fat would return to engulf everything in its path.

My part in the play was this doctor who doesn't want to let Elizabeth Seton back into the U.S. when she first returned there after her husband had died in Italy. They had gone to Italy to try to see if the climate made his tuberculosis any better, but it didn't and he croaked. She did find out about being Catholic while she was over there.

My part was pretty much to be a dick, and not want to let the Setons back in the country because they might have had tuberculosis too, for all I knew. But Elizabeth Ann Seton (or Patty Pam Kiernan, in this case) stood there and pooh-poohed about how her father had been a doctor, and that when she was little she would go with him when he cared for the sick and poor immigrants on Ellis Island.

That's where I'm a doctor from, Ellis Island in New York, in the harbor where the Statue of Liberty is. I was supposed to get all touched by God when I witnessed Elizabeth Seton's holiness, etcetera, and saw all of her five little kids with runny noses. It was no wonder I first thought they had TB! But I ended up not only letting them in, but finding them a place to live, buying them bags of flour so they could make bread, and some other stuff.

Slim Mars played one of the four Americans who stroll around being narrators, while the rest of us who play characters changed the sets and acted out little situations behind the four Americans, like the medical examiners' room, a street vendors scene, and other New Yorky stuff.

The First American's first line was, "It's 1903. America wanted the world's tired and poor, and now she's getting them."

Every rehearsal started off badly. Slim was quiet and always got nervous about being the first one in the play who had to speak, especially after Sister Ted had delivered her ten-minute death sentence to everyone about how today's rehearsal was the most important one (since yesterday's, anyway), and how it wasn't just about whether you had talent, but also about whether you were a good Catholic. And that was why she, Sister Ted, would be watching everyone carefully, and about how each rehearsal just might have a big impact on a student's religion and English grade.

So it always took twenty minutes at rehearsals just to get the damn thing started. Also, at the run-throughs, the girls doing costumes, sets, and publicity had kept charging into the wing to update Sister Ted about every button they sewed, or how the Donut House wanted to put an ad in the program, or how the ship's prow made out of cardboard had developed a big tear right where the anchor hole was supposed to be, and should they fix it with a tape on the inside or on the outside? These delays and interruptions also fried Slim's brain, in addition to his nervousness and the fact that his wrist was bare.

A really old nun who didn't teach anymore and just did odd jobs for the other nuns sat at the back of the auditorium with a script. She was the prompter. The problem was she couldn't hear very well, and she had this thick Baltimore accent, so you could barely understand her words if she did happen to say them loud enough to float down to the front of the auditorium. So all in all she really wasn't much help. By the time Sister Deadweight had figured out that one of us had gotten a line wrong, and found the correct one, and raised her voice loud enough to be heard, we were already a half-page further into the play.

I don't have to tell you how much confusion there was, but Sister Ted never seemed more happy than right then, when all the Seton activity was swirling around her, and there was no time to finish any one job. She would just poke whatever kid was standing in front of her in the ribs, and tell him to move it, then turn around and face the next question.

With pins in her mouth, and hemming a dress, she could still coach Bartos Cuscusmontrous on how to say the words "clipper ship."

Gleeper sheep.

Clih-purr ship!

May 20, 1975. Opening and closing night. A day that I will never be able to forget. They had brought out all the nuns from the convent, including the old ones who never came out, and could only be visited by the first grade, because they were so old they would get spazzed out by the little rat-faced rugrats who liked getting their dirty hands all over everything, which was a description of most of the younger grades. The old nuns stayed inside the convent and sewed and knitted and prayed pretty much full-time. That's how they earned their way. They were all sitting in front, like a telephone wire full of black crows. They had the first grade sitting with them on their folding chairs, and on the floor right at their feet. That meant we'd have to say our lines over all the little chattering, because kids that little didn't know what a play was, and that you were supposed to be quiet and listen to it. They thought everything was real. If somebody near them talked, they talked back.

Before the curtains opened Sister Ted gave us a big speech about how we had to act with the Holy Spirit, because it was a Holy Thing, the play, and we all had the Spirit, which I guess just shows that the Holy Spirit didn't choose the richest person in the world or the most handsome. The Holy Spirit just picked whoever the hell He wanted to, basically. There's nothing worse than God-squad lingo, where everything's a miracle and God jumps you every time you heist a cookie or aren't completely chock-full of gooey love just for a split second.

I saw Slim pacing around on stage behind the drawn curtain. I was in the wings standing next to my little doctor's desk, which later tripled as Seton's writing desk, when she was keeping her journal and writing down stuff about her Vocation to ditch her husband and kids and become a nun, and as the altar-table in the final scene. Slim knew about the sabotage but refused to participate. As a matter of fact, he wanted to tell Sister Ted as soon as Peter and I told him, but I used the usual threat, that I would ask his parents if I could borrow this cool book Slim had showed me.

You know, Mr. Mars, the one with the picture of the naked woman with a crescent moon tied to her face.

Slim always knuckled under to that one.

I had to push the desk onstage when I made my entrance. Slim was walking around and jiggling his arm. Sister Ted had made him take off his watch for the performance, but he kept looking for it. He was mumbling some weird thing to himself every time he looked for it and then looked away, like Must be two freckles after a hair by now.

Then the curtain was pulled, which Sister Ted always did herself, her big white baggy arms flapping above her head, her saggy muscles swinging back and forth like two little white cows. In rehearsals, by the time the swishing ringing noise made by the opening curtain had faded away, Slim was already paralyzed with nervousness. Sister Ted had told him to wait five seconds in complete silence before he started his first speech, after which the other three strolling Americans came waltzing out to tell their parts of the story.

Five seconds, which normally is not much time at all, is an eternity if you're nervous, and it's even longer if you're basically a watch-person deep down, and you're not allowed to wear your watch. Slim would always wait either one second, and begin his speech too fast, or he would wait fifteen seconds, and speak so slowly you would think he had just eaten a bag of sourdough pretzels and not washed them down. In fact, the rebellion during the The Mother Seton play didn't go well at all. I have to be honest: I was the weak link in the chain. Sometimes I go to pieces in public situations, ever since this time when I was eight and Emmet was four, and I truth-or-dared him to walk into a cocktail party my ma was having with his boner hanging out of the front of his Woody Woodpecker pjs.

"After her husband's death in Italy," the Second American was saying, "Elizabeth Seton returned to New York and wasted no time. The Catholic friends she had made in Italy had had a strong influence on her."

"She was received into the Catholic Church in 1805," said the Third American.

"But her Baptism led to estrangement from her family," the Fourth American said, "and her friends deserted her one by one. That left her and her children with reduced finances. And when Elizabeth formed her first school using the parlor of the house as a classrom, it marked the beginning of the Catholic parochial school system in the United States."

Peter and I had discussed it, and figured out that that was the single worst thing about Elizabeth Ann Seton, that she had created Catholic Schools. So that was the place we would start our sabotage.

There was supposed to be all this fake applause from the people on stage when the Second American announced that she was creating parochial schools, followed by Eddie Claypool canonizing Seton. Before Eddie did that, Peter was supposed to do a black-out, I was supposed to do a Fat Albert *Hey hey hey!*, then Peter would shine the spotlight.

Instead, Peter did the black-out, and I missed my cue. Eddie Claypool was confused, so he jumped in with his part.

Bwaapppp! it went, as he crushed the fart-pillow onto the floor of the stage.

The spotlight came on Eddie briefly as he was trying to rip open his vest, which was safety-pinned closed. By then everybody was screaming and shouting because it was so dark. By the time Peter got the light on Eddie, Sister Ted had already gotten Peter by the ear and was flapping her elbow up and down, like she was loosening up Peter's ear like a stuck nail. Peter had dropped down to one knee and was begging for mercy. Somebody flipped the house and stage lights back on. Patty Pam threw a forearm at Eddie Claypool, who then punched her on the side of her head and kicked out her ankle. She went down like a circus tent. Bartos burst into tears. Slim ran off stage and put his watch on.

We screwed it up, for sure. It wasn't exactly clear what we had done, besides mess up the lights. Probably anybody who didn't know better would have thought it was just a stage crew mess-up.

And it was mostly because I missed my cue. The trouble was I had been staring at Maxine Myna. She was in the audience smiling at me. I forgot to cue Peter. Then one of the little kids from the second grade laughed, and it sounded just like Fat Albert, and Eddie Claypool got mixed up and opened his shirt, and ended up looking like a spastic streaker.

What I saw was her hair, Maxine's hair. I had never seen it close up until we made out, when there were these long periods where we were just hugging. You can't make out without stopping for a breather every once in a while. But we never even separated for the breathers, really, we just hugged tightly like we were trying to choke each other.

My face was buried in her hair. I could see all the different colors in it. Knowing that about her, that she had those colors in there, that not everybody knew about, made me happier than anything else, happier than tongue and tits and holding hands, happy because I could keep looking at it and never get to the end of it.

I got so happy staring at Maxine while I was standing on stage twirling a stethoscope around, that I felt like I was in *Butterflies Are Free*, this movie with Goldie Hawn. She played this ditzy actress who had three stepfathers, and Edward Albert played this blind guy who'd never done anything fun in his whole life, and they got it on. Then his mother showed up. She didn't like Goldie Hawn because she thought she was a scuzz. The mother tried to describe to Eddie Albert how he was living like a pig, but he didn't care, because Goldie was always walking around in her underwear. He knew *that* for a fact because he felt her up every once in a awhile. The whole deal was fine by him. Plus, he was blind so he couldn't really see all of the mess in the apartment.

When I thought about *Butterflies Are Free*, I knew that all my problems—the sea urchins and Maxine, the fact that Sister Ted hated me and wanted me excommunicated, that my ma frowned at me and I frowned at my father because he was an alcoholic—none of it really mattered, because some day I would forget all about all of it.

Eventually Goldie Hawn dicks the blind guy around, near the end, but she sure gave him something to remember first.

I couldn't forget Maxine's hair because there was too much of it and every bit of it was different. There was orange and red and dark brown and a little blonde and some straw-looking hair, and her head underneath all that hair was pure white, like a baby's skin. In the one split second I was supposed to be thinking about something else—my lines, and the plan with Peter—I saw Maxine's hair and it looked almost red. It was practically glowing. In that split second I swear I forgot everything I was ever supposed to remember.

In the end, we had to do the whole canonization scene all over again, with Sister Ted standing behind Eddie Claypool and punching him in the kidneys when he stumbled on a line. Somehow we finished the play. Oscar Claypool came up on stage afterward.

"Simply brilliant, chaps. You couldn't have picked a better time for your sabotage. It went off like a charm."

"Screw off, Oscar," I told him. He was bigger than me but I didn't care. I felt like a horse's patooey and I didn't need some play fag in a scarf laughing at me.

Slow and Stupid Wins The Race

We broke in on Friday night because we thought Way Gross only stayed late to wax the floors on Thursday nights. All we had to do was avoid him, but all he seemed to do was sleep at his desk, which was way over on the other side of the building, in the hallway near the library. It was March 20, exactly one week before Good Friday. We had a great excuse for being at school at night, because we had gotten the job of guards for the Sodality Plant Sale. All these plants and flowers had been unloaded from a truck into the parking lot right behind the church on Friday afternoon. The plant sale was Saturday, during the day, so the head of Sodality wanted us out there with the stuff overnight, so it wouldn't get ripped off. It was still only March, but it had gotten freakishly warm. (That would all change in April, when it got freakishly cold. It's been a freakish year. Don't ask me why.)

We had some dirt on Way Gross, so weren't too worried about him anway. He had been the janitor at school for two years, and he was actually from Honduras. He seemed nice at first, but he definitely came with a heavy order of grease, and he turned out to be a real maggot in the end. His front tooth was gold. He wore pants a couple sizes too big, with a tight belt, because he was a cheap Catholic. Maybe he thought he was going to get bigger now that he was living in America and eating more. His real name was Chiquesas Huegros. The first year he was here, everyone called him Chick, but then the nuns had a meeting and they decided he should be respected, and called Mr. Huh-way Gras. So now we call him Mr. Way Gross.

You see, back on January 24, Peter Kiernan and I were walking back to class after 11 AM Mass. The eighth grade went to 11 AM Mass every Friday. It was the feast day of St. Francis DeSales, who besides being a famous Saint just for being holy was also the Patron Saint of the Hearing Impaired, because he let a young deaf guy live in his house and made up a sign language for talking with him way before there was even supposed to be such a thing as sign language.

We had this job of selling Cokes left over from the hot dog lunches. We'd wheel this milkcart around selling Cokes and opening the bottles for people, and since we had to end up back in the cooler room to unload, we had a great excuse for getting back late all the time.

"What took you so long?" Sister Ted said the first day we did it.

"We were putting stuff away," I told her. Actually, we had been sitting on top of the cooler drinking about eight free Cokes apiece, talking about some sort of bull-crap in the milkroom. One window into the milkroom had a broken latch, which Peter had discovered one day when we went in there with a couple of stink bombs and chucked one out the window. It had hit a speed bump, which then became one stinky speed bump.

On this particular day, when we came running out of the cooler room, since we were already late, we heard this sound.

"What's that?" Peter said. The sound was coming from the little bucket-room between the milk cooler room and the girl's bathroom. The door wasn't closed all the way. The sound was weird. We argued afterward about how to imitate it right.

"It was like this cooing noise, like a bird," said Peter Kiernan. He growled in the back of his throat.

"It was more of a grunting, like by someone skinny," I made up.

Since we were right there and we were already late we peeped through the crack of the bucket-room door. Peter went first and I kinda looked over his shoulder. We didn't say anything. Way Gross was on a ladder leaning against the wall peering through a vent with his pants down to his ankles and these little gold underpants on. We took off right then, before he had a clue we were there, we thought.

"He's a peeping Tom," I said when we got around the corner.

We had gotten a key to the kitchen in the back of the Church hall from Monsignor Bronk, and we were supposed to bring our sleeping bags in there, if it got too cold to stay outside with the plants. I worried about running into Sister Ted in the school. All the nuns in the convent went in and out of the school at strange hours, if they needed something. But Peter said not to worry. Also, we had a run-in with Rod Shivers, this Scottish guy who had lived in a little house near the rectory since before they even <u>built</u> the rectory or the church. The parish tried to make him scram when they broke ground, but Mr. Shivers whined like crazy and showed Monsignor Bronk this bogus little shrine to the Blessed Mary that he had put up in his backyard, when his wife died a hundred million years ago. (Darwin Mars called the shrine The Virgin on the Half-Shell.) So they had to let him stay, and from then on he was the groundskeeper for the parish, like it was a golf course

They should not have let him slide, because it made ol' Rod think he owned the place. Peter and I had found out that the rumor was true that he kept a shotgun loaded with rock salt by his shed door. Before midnight, which was when we were going to break into the school, we had been screwing around, carrying orchid plants over our heads as we marched past Mr. Shivers's house, singing as loud as we could:

> *Brother what a night it really was*
> *Brother what a fight it really was.*
> *The Night Chicago Died!*

Mr. Shivers stepped outside his door, pointed his double-barrel in the air, and let it blast.

"Ye rotten little weans!"

I looked at my feet as we ran like the blazes. I had these crappy desert boots on that looked like they were made out of gray cardboard. They had little blotches all over them where stuff had been spilled. There was root-beer, piss, rain, milk, gravy, and toothpaste down there. But the desert boots just smelled like my feet, which was a really bad odor.

We had ourselves a strange night, sitting there on top of our sleeping bags, guarding plants, and waiting for midnight. At midnight we would slip through the window with the broken latch in the milkroom.

The lights in the parking lot behind the church were bright, and really high up, so weird shadows of leaves and wires and flying trash were whipping around above the bushes. The basketball nets were made out of chain, and I could hear them clashing together in the wind.

At St. Tabasco, we had to say the Sorrowful Mysteries of the Rosary every Friday during Lent. The Sorrowful Mysteries are The Agony in the Garden, the Scourging at the Pillar, The Crowning with Thorns, The Carrying of the Cross, and the Crucifixion and Death. Peter and I talked about the time we had made the cross for the Passion Play at school, because there are themes for all the separate Mysteries, and the theme for the Carrying of the Cross was Perserverance and Strength. We agreed that we both felt pretty strong after carrying the cross all the way down Boiling Brook Parkway to the school, since it was heavy, and people honked at us as if we were psychos.

The strangest theme for a Mystery is for the Scouring at the Pillar, because its themes are Modesty and Purity. We couldn't figure why standing there with your hands tied to a marble pillar getting the hide whipped off your back was supposed to make you modest. Then we decided to get on with what we had to do.

Some of the rooms in the school were locked, like the offices. The nuns had been talking about locking up the classrooms too, because supplies had been disappearing, but they hadn't done it yet. We walked down the hallways. I felt so nervous that I thought I had to pee, but it just came out of my body as sweat, because pretty soon I didn't have to pee anymore. When we walked past the front of the school, where Sister Skeletona's office and the nurse's office were, a car drove by on Boiling Brook. For a split second we were lit up by the headlights, right underneath the Cardinal's picture by the main door.

When the headlights shined in, I could see into this old trophy case up there. There was an old leather football in it that looked like a big cow crap, and there was a state schoolboy's championship trophy with Danny Dens's name right at the top of the plaque. He had been team captain that year. He shot 69 percent from the field and made eight free throws in the final game.

I had only been in the fifth grade so I flipped out about the whole thing. After the game I waited in a crowd near the locker-room doors. When Danny walked by, I tried to squeeze up to the front. We didn't really know each other very well, but he was pretty nice.

"Dann-EEE! Dan The Man!" I yelled, but he didn't see me. I tried to talk to him about the championship once when we shot around, but he said he didn't think about it anymore.

"But it must have made you feel great! You were a hero. You won the game. I would be thinking about it constantly"!

Danny Dens looked at me. "It was just a game," he said. I fed him a few alley-oops, and then it was dinner time, thank God. It had gotten so quiet that I thought he hated me.

Danny Dens was only 5'10", but he had big shoulders, so he played guard. At least that's what he told me. His father would sit outside their house in a white T-shirt and long pants, and coach him while we shot around. I think Mr. Dens was glad I was there because that meant he didn't have to stand under the bucket, and rebound, and pass it back out so Danny could just keep shooting. Stay low on your dribble, Mr. Dens would say. Danny would stop, walk back up to the top of the key, and try it again, the right way.

Danny always wore a University of Maryland sleeveless jersey and cut-off sweats, even in February when there was still a little frost on the ground. I'll work up a sweat, and then I won't feel the cold, he told me. His feet were Size Twelves, and his sneakers always had orange laces in them. He was a cool guy, and still nice. I just wanted to be nice like he was nice. It really was a little too late for me to turn into a basketball hotshot. But if his dad wasn't out there, Danny let me shoot for every time he took a shot, and it wasn't because he wanted to coach me, or tell me I was bad, or to just plain deal on me. He wanted to talk about other things while we played.

Emmet's homeroom was insane. The desks were all too small, and there was a little circle of tiny chairs around the phonograph in the back corner. I shined my massive flashlight up the wall behind the phonograph, and there was a big poster hanging up there that said "Our Friend The Ear." Then I shined it on the train clock, and down.

I sat down on one of the tiny chairs, and my thighs smacked up into my chest. In front of me, Peter stood on top of the shelf and started taking down the clock. We'd steal that. That would be our big accomplishment. We both knew it at the same time. Then we heard a little scratching noise against the glass. We froze like little baby rabbits.

Way Gross was looking in through the window from the outside, but we could tell his eyes hadn't adjusted very well, and he couldn't see us yet. He was scanning back and forth across the room, like a pirate with a spyglass. I quickly switched off the flashlight. We sat and waited for a few minutes.

"He musta seen it," Peter whispered. As I stood up, the chair I had been sitting in broke, and I fell over backward and smacked the top of the phonograph (it was the kind that had a hinge and a latch). The top opened up and flipped back against the window, and the window cracked.

"Let's get outa here!" Peter hissed. We quickly slipped back out the way we came, but when we tore by the supply room, the door was half-open. We could see Way Gross was in there with his back to the door. He was poking around under the shelves. I stumbled and smacked against the door, and it slammed shut.

When we got outside the building, we could hear Way Gross calling out from the storeroom, through one of those little steel ventilator fans that has a chain hanging down from it. We doubled back to where he had first looked in at us when we were in Emmet's homeroom, and we found all these bottles of Boones Farm Strawberry Wine under there and a blanket. I sneaked up to the supply room fan and tried to look in, but couldn't see anything.

Peter did his hyena laugh. "How-oo how-oo how-oo!"

"Geh me ouda heere!" Way Gross shouted.

"No way. Not until you promise us you're not going to tell on us!"

"I no what you tocking about."

"Maybe we'll put these bottles of wine on the principal's chair, and then when they come find you in the morning, you're out of luck."

We waited. I could hear Way Gross breathing on the other side of the fan.

"Okay, tough guy," Peter said to him. "You can think about it a little bit tonight since you're not going anywhere."

❖ ❖ ❖

My ma waited a whole day to even get to stare at me through all of dinner time. I know what that was about: she always knew when I'd done

something wrong, even when she didn't know what it was. It was super-
natural.

She let me cool my jets almost until bedtime on Saturday. I had to
help Maud do the dishes while she sat at the kitchen table and wrote
checks. She didn't say anything. Then I did homework in my room with
the door open and her right across the hall with Molly, getting her ready
for bed. Then we all watched TV for a half-hour. Nothing. My ma wasn't
even looking at me anymore. I thought I might be safe.

But instead, when I was in bed, and Emmet was already asleep, and
I had just turned out the light, she came in and gave me the Vague
Speech. This time, though, it was Vaguely Good. She told me things
worked out if you gave them time, and that she was raising her children
to be good themselves, not to take orders like robots. Then she kissed me
on the hair and walked out.

We had been inside the school for what seemed like hours, and I had
gotten the third degree when I got home the next morning. My ma was
just getting off the phone. She had heard there had been a burglary
reported at school. Way Gross had been screaming out curses all night
long.

My ma had said to me—That poor janitor was locked up in a closet
by the burglars.

—We didn't hear anything, I said. I opened the refrigerator door and
ducked my head down underneath the salad crisper, which seemed to be
a good place to go when I was feeling guilty.

—Well, that seems strange, my ma said. She scootched Molly back up
to the kitchen table and set up a little Dixie glass of water in front of her.
My ma is no dummy, but she's busy thinking of a lot of other stuff more
than me most of the time, thank God.

The following Monday at school was tense. Of course, Peter and I
were immediately enormous suspects, because of Peter's long record of
attacking St. Tabasco and my long history of going along with people.
Way Gross reported all the strange sounds and the flashlight. Of course,
he made up a lot of other crap to cover his own tracks. The cops had
found blood on the floor because I got a piece of glass caught between my
fingers. It had just been a small cut, but in ten seconds my hand was

sticky with all the blood. All in all, we had been pretty messy.

You know that feeling when you're just about to get caught doing something? Naturally you don't. Nobody does. That's why everybody gets caught a lot of the time. But somehow this time we had lucked out. So slow and stupid won the race.

It was the beginning of Holy Week. I was in one of the classes that Sister French had taught—music class—and my ma was the substitute. Things weren't going too well, because she was trying real hard to follow Frenchie's stupid class plan that said that on that day we were supposed to listen to a recording of the William Tell Overture, which is okay as far as music goes, even though it's more fun to sit there and think about him shooting an apple off of somebody's head and missing by just a little and skewering the dude so that his skull was pinned to the tree he was leaning against, like an empty big bladder.

So my ma is fumbling along trying to find the right groove on the scratchy old William Tell album, and some of the jocks are giving her crap, because they want to see if they can get old Digby's ma steamed up right in front of everybody and then rank on me later about it.

"Miziz Shaw, Miziz Shaw," Frank Wharsit moaned.

"What is it, Frank?"

"Are we going to sing?"

"No, we are going to listen to the William Tell overture and then we are going to study how an overture is constructed."

"But Sister French always let us sing!" Frank Wharsit was about 5'10" and weighed 160 pounds. He had the weird habit of constantly licking his thumbs and then jamming them onto his sideburns and plastering them down. He got up from his desk, taking about half of it with him, and wandered up the aisle to the desk. My ma was standing off to the side where the record player was. She saw him. She straightened up and put her hands on her hips and smiled.

I knew that look. It wasn't happy. It didn't even look happy. If you blocked her little smile out of your head, you could see she was thinking about what to do next. Frank just wandered up to the desk and picked up the pitch pipe that was lying there and started tooting on it like he was the Pied Piper. Then the door burst open and Monsignor Bronk and the principal Sister Skeletona marched in.

"Mr. Wharsit, what are you doing out of your seat?" Sister Skeleton screeched at him.

"I was just—"

"I'm sorry, Sister, but I had asked Frank to bring me my pitch pipe. We were just about to start a sing-a-long." Frank shot my ma a grateful look, then lumbered over and handed her the pitch pipe.

Sister Skeletona stared out at the rest of us like we were ants marching one by one down into a drainpipe. "There was a break-in last Friday night here at the school. It is a very serious situation."

"Some of your parents have been calling in today," Monsignor Bronk said. "Apparently students have been telling them the wildest rumors. Please reassure them the blood that was found on the floor of Mr. Man's classroom was *not* gorilla blood, Mr. Huegros was *not* tortured, and we will continue to have regular classes all week, since it will *not* be necessary for the FBI to come in and dust the entire fourth grade for fingerprints."

I kept my eyes straight ahead looking at my ma, who was not looking at me.

Monsignor cleared his throat. "Mrs. Shaw, you have assured me already that you have spoken to your son about this, since he may have seen or heard something at the time of the break-in".

"I have, Monsignor. Digby told me as soon as he got home the next morning that they had heard glass breaking, but he and Peter Kiernan thought it would be wiser just to sit tight where they were, under those lights, that maybe it was just the wind. It was windy Friday night, Monsignor. I can certainly say that Digby would have the sense to let the police handle it if it was something happening."

"Yes, yes." Monsignor clearly didn't believe her, or at least thought that I shouldn't be believed. "Well, that backs up what Mr. Huegros has said about that night, even though the poor man is under a great deal of stress because of his abduction."

Monsignor Bronk went on to say that the police still figured it had been students who broke in, since nothing was stolen, as far as they could tell. We'd walked right past a reel-to-reel tape recorder that Emmet's class had earned by bringing in more Dinty Moore Beef Stew can labels than anybody else in the universe. This little rat named Calvin in Emmet's class organized a team that went up to the grocery store, sliced the labels off a whole bunch of cans, then put the bare cans way in the back of the shelves and pushed some more of the labeled cans up front. Come to think of it, that wasn't too shabby, but the guy was a thug. Emmet should have been terrified of him, but instead he fed him answers in class, and laughed at his farts.

We didn't even look through desks, or break into the A/V Room and pour water on stuff. This confused Monsignor Bronk, but he was still determined to bust whoever it was, and make sure they thought that they were going straight to hell.

"Thank you for letting us interrupt your class time, Mrs. Shaw," Sister Skeletona said. "I assume Sister Ted has told you about the special faculty meeting after school today."

"Yes, Sister Skeletona. I will be attending."

I got a sinking feeling in my stomach. My ma was now *working* for Sister Ted. Monsignor and Sister Skeleton turned to leave, and Patty Pam Kiernan jumped out of her seat.

"Monsignor, may we have your blessing?" Any time Monsignor was around, you could count on the biggest brownie in the class to bounce up and ask him to do his spell.

"Of course." Monsignor barely looked at us as he kung-fooed out a blessing.

Emmet

It's hard to describe someone if he won't look at you. Emmet went through a phase where he never looked at me when he spoke because he was hoping he didn't have to say anything else, since I had set up this tricky new routine for hitting him that was impossible to beat.

Okay, Emmet, you understand? I will only hit you, if you say something, or you don't say something.

What? he would say quickly, but pretty carefully, just to have some time to think about what I meant. WHONK! he'd get a punch.

Now *you* can hit *me.* If you don't hit me, I'll have to hit you, and if you do hit me, I'll have to hit you for me. WHONK! The rules didn't make any sense, and Emmet always ended up getting hit for anything he did or said, or didn't do or didn't say, so now he tried to walk along the wall when he saw me, as if he had suction pads on his hands, like a tree frog.

That's why sometimes Emmet and I have to spend some special time together. I just tie him up on a bar stool.

I know it sounds cruel, but it was one of Emmet's weird gifts. He could get out of being tied up very tight with several different ropes, and he loved doing it. Sometimes it took him hours. He wiggled his tiny muscles for long minutes to stretch out the rope. Sometimes he bit at the knots to soften them up. I thought that would make them dry back even tighter, but Emmet corrected me once, when I asked him.

"I don't let them dry. If I'm biting one, I keep biting it until I can undo it."

Emmet lets me do other human experiments on him. Once I had

fainted him. It was Raft Night at the pool we belonged to, and on Raft Night everybody brought in their rafts (duh) that they took to the beach in the summer, so almost the whole surface of the pool was covered with rafts. You really couldn't try any surfing moves like you could at the beach, so that was bogus, but you could do great tortures on little kids, by paddling after them and covering their heads with your rafts and not letting them come up for any air. The lifeguards put the bright lights on. Everybody was screaming like it was Doomsday.

Before we got in the water, Emmet and I went into the men's locker rooms. You didn't really get a locker, you got a little white wooden square on the wall. You had to take a shower before you went in the water, in case you had crap on you someplace. Sometimes, we had a sword-fight in there where you cross your pee-streams like blades. If you kept the shower going, the pee got washed down pretty quickly. I fainted Emmet in the shower. I grabbed him from behind and locked my arms lightly around his chest. Then I counted and made him take ten deep breaths, and hold the tenth one. As he was holding it, I squeezed his chest really hard. He passed out and went down like a ton of bricks and cracked his head. He was laying in the water for a couple of seconds, so I thought he was completely dead, but then he jumped up to his feet. I had never seen Emmet ever jump before. He pointed at the shower heads and said "Look at the giraffes!" which was pretty freaked out of him to do, so I had to give him credit.

If I tied him up, I was always friendly. I smiled a lot, because it was always hilarious to see Emmet's skinny arms straining and struggling with the rope. We have an old stool in our bedroom that doesn't go anywhere else in the house. Some rope was hidden in my closet. I would be in deep doo-dah for tying Emmet up, if my ma ever found out. But like I said, Emmet loved doing it so much that he never ratted on me. Sometimes he'd even fall off the stool, trying to work the cords free, and from the floor he'd ask me to put him back on the chair, so he could get back to work on the knots.

This time I tied him as tight as I could without cutting off his circulation. I wrapped one rope around his body and arms, and then I passed it under his legs and back around behind his neck. That's what the Japs do to the two American prisoners of war in the movie, *Too Late The Hero*, before they start really torturing them and hanging them from meathooks.

When I had tied Emmet up, I lay back on my bed and looked at him pretty close, and I wondered if I looked that messed up when I was little. These were some of my discoveries. He had different-colored eyes. There were other ways of describing him, like that he had a long, red-peach-colored tongue, and that one of his teeth was turned almost all the way to the side, but once you saw his eyes, that's all you really remembered about him. The right eye was gray, and the left one was blue, but light blue, like you could have seen through it if it had been water, instead of being an eye.

Once I told him, "You look like a robot that should be sent back to the factory." They were big, too, and not just the eyeholes. His eyeballs stuck out like there was something behind them, pushing them out. Maybe that was why they were strong. Emmet was always seeing more to be nervous about up ahead or on the ground, or above his head and slightly over him.

The little red punctuation marks, like little periods in little circles in the very corners of his eyes, were bigger than they should be. At least that's what I thought, but what did I know? I had squinty pig-eyes, and so did Maud, so when we blinked it was hard to see it. Emmet didn't really even blink at all, because a blink was not supposed to make any noise. But when Emmet opened and closed his eyes, you heard this little click.

Emmet's hair was always cut in a straight line across his forehead. My hair was cut the same way, since we usually went to the barbershop at the same time. But I hate to feel the hair in a little wall across my forehead. It drives me crazy. So I'm constantly shoving my fingers up my forehead and grabbing the clump of hair that makes up the bangs, and then sweeping it over to the left side, like I'm yanking back a little curtain.

There was also a freckle on top of Emmet's head that you could only see if the wind was blowing. It was a light fleshy color, and pretty big, but it was easy to forget about that, too. Then, when you saw it again, you remembered how weird Emmet was.

I watched him start to do his stuff. Emmet started rocking back and forth slowly, testing to see the kind of job I did. After a while he gave me this silly little grin. That meant he had started. I read for about ten minutes. Then I said, "So, Emmet, your homeroom is ten, isn't it?"

"Yeah. Between nine and eleven."

Duh, I thought to myself. "You know, I think I was in homeroom ten back when I was in fourth grade."

"You were in nine."

"How do you know that?"

"Because I have your old Science book. It says 'Room nine' next to your name."

We sat there quietly. Emmet was stretching his neck against the noose around his neck. I went over to him. A bit of the rope had worked up above his collar and was chafing his neck, so I tucked it back below his collar.

"Thanks," Emmet whispered.

"I remember homeroom ten. It's the one that has the big fake clock that looks like a locomotive in the cloakroom, isn't it?" I was running a stopwatch, which made me feel a little bit like Slim Mars, but Emmet kept a list in his *My Book About Me* of the different times it took for him to get free when he got tied up. He also had a coding system for how difficult the knots were.

"Yeah. The one with the clock."

Emmet was off in another world. He had worked one leg free, and he was doing little knee flexes with it to loosen the manacle knot I had fastened around his waist. I waited another five minutes and chewed on a hangnail.

Emmet had now gotten his neck free, and was leaning over at the waist snapping his teeth at the knots on his hands. He was more than halfway done already.

More time passed, I guess. I looked up when Emmet fell off the stool with a little grunt and started writhing around on the floor.

"Do you want back up?" I asked him. (Sometimes he likes lying on his side and working the ropes a little bit from that angle.)

"Yeah." I picked him up and put his butt back on the stool.

One last thing about Emmet. His breath was totally non-smelly. I know because I've pounded him enough times, straddling him with my legs, where his mouth was open because he was trying to breathe while I was choking the stuffing out of him. A little of his breath would go whistling up into my face and under my hair, and I'd stop breathing through my nose automatically. I told you I hate bad breath worse than almost anything. But pretty soon my nose would get curious, and open up again a little, to test the air above Emmet's mouth, and then there would be no smell at all, no matter what. I can sit across from him at breakfast when we eat bacon, and not a single smell of it will be on his breath. It's a little bit whacked, like everything else about Emmet. Meanwhile, I ooze smells out of my pores. When I eat bacon, I basically smell like a slaughterhouse.

The only other time I really pay attention to Emmet is when I'm helping him with his homework. Once I was having dinner alone, because I had got back too late. My ma had put it out. It was a pot pie. The hot gravy that had snuck out of the sides of the crust and bubbled up through the fork-holes had dried out and was hard, like snot. I yelled for Emmet as I started eating. I poked at my pot pie and found some soft parts, so I carved it up a little bit. It was a pretty simple dinner.

Emmet came in very sadly dragging his book bag and sat down across from me. He rested his forehead on his arm, which was streaked with about eight out of ten of his pen colors.

A Band Aid was on his knee and covered a scab that he got when he was trying to hide from a fifth grader who had been walking toward him with a knife.

"What sort of knife?" I had asked Emmet.

"A Swiss Army knife," Emmet said. "I could see it hanging from a loop of his belt."

"Well, people who are going to stab you don't usually do it with a Swiss Army Knife," I said. Emmet looked at me and nodded his head slowly. It was enough to make me feel like a real big brother. But I'm sure it didn't last long.

Emmet waved a piece of mimeograph paper at me. I took it and began reading automatically to him. "List seven things that you love to do," I droned. "Next to each entry write the date you did it last. Place an A or a P next to each entry—do you like to do it alone or with other people?"

I stopped reading because this big whistling noise had come from Emmet. It was like he was sighing and yawning at the same time. "Emmet, what the hell class is this homework from?"

Emmet looked like his neck had fallen asleep. "Religion," he whispered.

I looked at it again. "Place a dollar sign next to each entry that requires money," I read. "Place an * next to the five you like to do most. Check the items that would not have been there two years ago. Circle those that might not be there five years from now."

I had thought that it was going to take hours, but twenty minutes later we were done, because I made up half of them. Emmet really got excited about doing it, after I had made up the first five. He was thinking real hard, but I only wrote down every other thing he said, because he took too long. When Emmet was remembering something he sat very still with this soft look on his face. It was like he could see things in his brain moving in front of him. He said Oh! a lot, too. Sometimes he talked to what he saw.

Emmet had weird friends, too. His best friend Johnny went around to all the houses in the neighborhood knocking on the doors. Then Johnny asked the mother of the house if he could play with her vacuum cleaner.

My what?

Your vacuum cleaner. We have an upright that has a front light, and bag indicator that only comes on when the bag is full of dust.

Well, why don't you go play with that?

I already *did*. I want to see *yours*. *Please* can't I see yours?

This is what our list looked like:

1. Play with my three friends. 11/29. P.
2. Play Baseball. Last year some time. P.
3. Sing. Yesterday. A & P. *
4. Explore. 2 months ago. P. (You have to remember that Emmet calls anything he does while he has shoes on "exploring.")
5. Rumble. Today. P. ("Rumble" meant Emmet got knocked down by someone.)
6. Pet dogs. A & P. * (The dog that humped Emmet's leg is gone. It opened the refrigerator by itself one day, ate four sticks of butter and ran away. Emmet does pet all the other dogs on the street, though.)
7. Eat cheese and pickles. A & P.
8. Talk with my brother in bed. P.

Sometimes we did talk in bed. Usually it was mostly Emmet talking. I was just trying to go to sleep, but he would mumble along for a long time and then say Digby? Digby? Can you hear me? I usually said Yes, if I wasn't too tired, but sometimes I felt mean and I didn't say anything, because I just wanted to go to sleep.

We finally finished his homework. We each folded up our pieces of paper and put them into our pockets. Then we nodded at each other, and Emmet beat it.

Another time Emmet was trying to be like Abe Lincoln when he was young, because he had read a book about him. Emmet emptied his desk out and brought all of his schoolbooks home every night. He would set them down by the fireplace and half-crouch, half-sit there studying after dinner. He even tried writing with a piece of burnt wood from the fireplace like Abe did, but he just made a mess, and after a couple of times, my father said, Can it.

Slim and I slinked in through the front door, and then we gunned it for the basement to watch *Count Gor De Vol's Mystery Horror Movie* on TV before dinner.

"Just a minute, Mister." Somehow, my father had sneaked in from work early, and his briefcase was under the piano. One of its snaps wasn't fastened. He was reading the newspaper in his chair, and the headline said HOFFA. A glass of iced tea and soda water with froth on it that looked like frog spawn sat on the table by his armchair. He didn't have a cocktail now, when he came home from work, because my ma had talked to him, and we heard them.

My father said, "I think your brother needs a little assistance."

Slim and I looked at each other with this really intense look.

"We have to do some work on a school project in the lab—" I started to say.

"You can give your brother a minute of your time. That won't kill you. Right, Solomon?"

Slim, because he was the weakest person alive, caved instantly. "Yeah, Mr. Shaw, okay!" He could have backed me and lied about something we had to do, but he didn't.

"Emmet has been really working hard to be like some president, and that's just fine by me. Now, you get over there and help him."

I heaved a sigh like I had just dumped a monster, because I was trapped. My father could care less what I wanted to do. Slim did whatever he was told to do by the oldest person around. And Emmet only liked to do the most boring things in the world. It was the kind of day I was having more and more often. My problem was that I was out there cruising around between several different projects at once, so people thought they could just stop me at any time and give me a new assignment. I cruise between my projects because I don't like to be caught working. It looks gay to work. I work secretly.

Jack of all trades is master of none, my ma would say when she looked into my room at the stacks of different projects: the dam with trees made out of sponges, my coin collection with all the holes in it, the crystal radio set, and the steam engine that ran on little pieces of fuel that looked like boullion cubes.

I had to change this sometime, but I couldn't right then. I was too lazy. I would just help Emmet, and get rid of Slim, and be forgotten by my father, then cruise by the Myna's and try to get lucky. I patted my pocket and felt my Binaca Blast in there, like a magic bullet.

Emmet had our family's enormous white Bible open right next to him on the bricks of the fireplace. The color paintings at the beginning of the Bible were cool. I used to check them out all the time when I was home from school sick, when I got scared that I just had to do something, or I would dry up and disappear. There's the picture of Abraham about to torch his son Whatshisface as a test. I always wondered, What if God had been one second too late? Abraham would have been completely teed off. The Jews might have been down the drain.

Sister Ted would say I was starting an argument just to hear myself talk for saying that about Abraham, but she can go suck an egg. Thoughts pop into your head, but they're your thoughts. You have to do something with them, or you'll just get stupider. Besides, I wasn't very logical when I was at home and had fever. I would always have this one dream about being in a long dark basement and having to move all of this heavy stuff, except it was too heavy and weighed me down, but I couldn't stop loading more on top of it, and then I couldn't breathe.

Emmet was reading about Joseph and his brothers, an okay story if you can skip the pretty gay coat stuff and go on to where he reads people's dreams. That's righteous. He was in jail, but he had dreams about the seven skinny cows, and then everybody knew he was talking about famine. One day the king had a dream and totally spazzed out, and Joseph told the king that his dream meant he was shit out of luck, and it turned out he was right. The king took a major loss the very next thing. Joseph got promoted from slave immediately, and got his brothers out of trouble, too.

Emmet was writing a book report on the Bible, for God's sake.

"Why did you pick the Bible?" I asked him. "Couldn't you have at least picked something shorter?"

"Mr. Man said we could pick *any book* we wanted," Emmet whispered.

My father was glaring at me. He had some iced tea froth on his upper lip. "For Christ's sake, Digby, can't you just _help_ him?"

"I *am* helping."

"Is he helping, Emmet?" my father asked.

Emmet looked at me and then he looked at him. It was not a great position to be in. "He's almost helping, Dad."

"Well, start helping *all the way*, Digby."

We would be stuck there forever. Slim was happy to sit on the rug because Maud had come in and he got to watch her play "Tocatta Brilliante" on the piano, which is a pretty jumpy piece of music.

We immediately got stuck on the table of contents for the book report. It went like this: Emmet called the chapter on Genesis "Starting Out," the chapter on Exodus "Leaving Home," and he'd also made up a title for the Book of Kings, which would be called "The Presidents of Religion." So, so far he seemed to have a pretty good idea going, and it wasn't too bad to sit with him while he tried to think of titles for really hard chapters like Nahum and Zephaniah.

I have Emmet's book report here in the scrapbook. I had to bargain with him to get it, because he wanted to hang on to it himself. I eventually gave him ten old Richie Rich comic books. I knew them inside and out, so it was no big loss. I wanted the book report, because I thought it was cool for old Emmet to take on the whole Bible all at once.

Another time I got stuck with Emmet and his homework, he had stopped trying to be Abe Lincoln. I mean, he still was doing his homework near the fireplace, but now he wanted to be a fireman.

He was really just into setting fires, which everybody tried at one time or another. I used to carry lighter fluid to Boy Scout meetings. Once we had had a camp-out and all the parents came for our campfire on the first night. I got to light the fire, since even the Scoutmaster knew I was the resident pyro, but I had to dress like an Indian, in a loincloth with no dees on, and my gonads were dangling like the littlest bunch of grapes that ever grew.

Emmet liked Ohio Blue-Tip matches. They're the kind you can strike anywhere. I showed him how to light one on the bottom of his upper middle tooth, by putting the very tip underneath the tooth and snapping it across the ridged part. I told him that he had to be quick, or he would burn his lips, and then he would eventually tell on me when he could finally speak again, and I would be busted and grounded because of his idiotness, and would have to hunt him down and kill him.

So that night Emmet was paying about 2 percent of his attention to his homework while I was helping. He kept patting his shirt pocket. When he leaned over the fireplace, I could see he had stored four Blue-Tips in the pocket to play with later on.

Emmet was in this thing call *The Reading Program*, for kids who were motivated by themselves to read. You wrote down all the books you had read on the cover of one folder, where you kept all your progress cards. Progress cards were tests you had taken when you were done with the book. They didn't have *The Reading Program* when I was in the fourth grade, which was too bad. I had secretly been reading a lot of Emmet's books in the bathroom. All you need is about one good plop and you're finished.

So far, Emmet had read *Steinmetz, Wizard of Light, Story of a Bad Boy, Binkie's Billions, Running Backs of the NFL, Avalanche Patrol, Go Away Ruthie,* and *The Witchcraft of Salem Village*. Not too shabby for a fourth grader. But on all of Emmet's answer cards the activities line was blank.

Why don't you ever do any of the activities? I asked him.

I don't like them.

Why?

I don't like them.

I already explained about how good Emmet was at repeating things.

❀ ❀ ❀

The only other interesting things about Emmet are all things that show how weird he is. We used to have this dog Happy that loved to hump Emmet's leg underneath the kitchen table. Happy loved to hump everybody's legs if it could, but Emmet was the one who was the most clueless, so at dinner, we'd see Happy dog edging around the corner from the dining room, looking for Emmet. Then he'd streak under the table, and two seconds later you'd hear it.

"Ma, Ma!" Emmet would be holding his spoon in front of him with some soup balanced in it.

"What, Emmet?"

"Happy is moe-ing my leg, Ma! He's moe-ing my leg!"

"Then push him away." A couple of minutes would go by.

"Happy's doing it again, Ma! He's doing it again."

And once my ma gave Emmet this book called *My Book About Me*, which had all these sentences in it with blanks left at the end of them. Emmet had to go around the house counting all our stuff, like how many lamps there were and how many windows, and then he wrote it down in the book. Some of it was funny, though, because Emmet thought nobody else in the world would ever look at it, so he wrote down all the stuff he would never say in public. I have grabbed it from him and read through the whole thing, and read the really gay parts out loud just to make him mad.

So it was not a big surprise one afternoon, when I stumbled over Emmet on his knees, with his gigantic pen in his hand, counting closets. Another time it had been faucets. He had already measured everything on his body—his height and weight constantly changed in the book.

"Can I ask you something?" Emmet asked me. I had plopped down on the sofa to read a book while watching *Green Hornet*, who was always pretty smooth and made you want to run outside and destroy somebody, even if he wasn't quite as cool as Ultraman, who was on next.

"What?"

"Those little doors in the bedroom—are they closets?"

"No. They're the under-the-eaves." Emmet looked disappointed, but he just opened the book and erased something, and then scribbled over it. He had a pen eraser, which as everybody knows works only a couple of times, and then starts erasing the paper along with the ink. Emmet had already changed his measurements for a hat, shoes, in-seam, waist, and his neck, which I can tell you right now is a size that I have no problem getting one hand around, from the many times I have had to threaten him with a good choke to get him to do what I say.

There were also whole pages in the book that had been left blank, where he was supposed to write about his vacations, what his room looked like, and what all the titles of his books were. He had managed to list his favorite sport (tetherball), food (meatballs), drink (Yoo-Hoo), TV Show (*Count Gore DeVol*), movie (*Chitty Chitty Bang Bang*), song ("Polly Wolly Doodle") and part of the body (knee).

It was like another humongous source of homework as far as I could tell, but Emmet didn't think so. I asked him why he worked so hard on it all the time.

"I want to write a book," he said, without looking at me.

Taylor Heddon was the tallest guy we knew. He was also Emmet's godfather. Emmet had gotten him to sign *My Book About Me* on the Tallest People page. Emmet had also made Molly step on a paint-can lid for her footprint on the Shortest People page. In the part of the book where you were supposed to make up your own story, Emmet had written this weird autobiographical thing that was a lot like our family, except in it Emmet was the oldest, not me, and he ordered me around and made me sleep outside in a tent when it was raining. That's what everyone does in their own story.

Still, sometimes he seemed like me in a good way, and sometimes he seemed like he was going to be an idiot in exactly the same ways I was too. Two years ago, Emmet had swept the entire second grade with his science fair project. My ma rented an incubator, and he hatched baby chicks. Out of twelve eggs, seven chicks survived. The project even made the local news.

But then last year, in third grade, Emmet's project was called "The Dancing Puppet." It was pretty sad. Emmet made a skinny stick-man out of paper clips, and then moved a magnet underneath a little cloth stage platform that the puppet hung down over. The puppet's clips rattled together and jerked around. Emmet played a tape of the song "Dance With Me," which Maud had picked out for him:

Dance with me
I want to be your partner
Can't you see
 The music is just starting
Night is falling, and I am calling
Dance with me.

The puppet was supposed to be dancing to it. It was lame, but it made me feel sort of bad too. I could laugh at it myself, no problem, but if I saw anyone else laughing, my face got red, and I felt like killing them. Emmet just sat next to his project, clicking his pen and scratching at the scab on his knee. Occasionally he would slip the pen under the patch and scratch with that, but then it started bleeding really badly, and he had to go to the nurse's office where they called my ma and she came to pick him up. He ended up in the emergency room getting two stitches on his knee, because he had scratched at it so badly.

Now that's an itch for you...

The Loser Party

One Sunday I visted Maxine at her babysitting job at the Rubys. They live between her house and my house. They only have one baby and he sleeps through the night. I had also babysat for them a couple of times. The Rubys owned a copy of *The Joy of Sex,* which had bogus charcoal sketches of naked people scrumping, on the highest bookshelf in their rumpus room. The cover jumped out at you like a tiger. Just being in that room sexed me out beyond belief.

They also had another book up there called *The Prisoner of Sex,* and it was by a raging pervert named Norman Mailer who stuck a crooked carrot up a girl's crack. I flipped through it pretty fast while Maxine was putting the baby to bed. The girl in the book was deaf and mute, so it was hard to figure out why he was trying to date her, exactly, but then again, I skipped over most of the beginning of the chapter so I could get to the dirty part. Dirty words stick out on the page. Usually you don't even have to look very hard. All of a sudden you're right in the middle of horny talk. Just keep your eyes peeled for a lot of exclamation points, and the word "she" used a lot, and you're usually getting pretty hot.

I have had only one real make-out before, like I said, with Maud's friend Margaret Grabaski. She made me swear I wouldn't tell Maud about it. I don't even know if that's how you really spell her last name, but that's what it sounds like. She kissed me down in our basement and she kept her eyes open while we were kissing. No tongue, but she did put my hand on her butt. Then her eyes got real wide and she stopped. "You look like Maud from really close up," Margaret said. "It's making me feel weird." So she got to stop feeling weird, but I got to start. My monster was totally confused and wouldn't back down for a long time.

The make-out with Maxine that night was much better. I had done a lot of the work already, in the wagon pulled by Ricky Seerser, and this make-out was another step forward, because at the Rubys' Maxine let me play inside with her tits. Also, Maud wasn't lurking around giving me the eye, like she had been after Margaret Grabaski left. Maud has a way of looking at me that made me think she knew what I was up to, and that she would be making a full report when the time came.

But what I happened to know about her was that she had a special pair of platform shoes she wore when she went to the dance with Rafe Biktor that my ma didn't know about. She kept them at her friend's house who she double-dated with, so when she left our house she had regular old brown shoes on, but then she changed. They were nose-bleed platforms. When you saw a girl wearing them you could smirk at her and say How's the air up there? I will be busting Maud big-time on that one if I hear a peep out of her any time soon.

At the Rubys', the coast was clear. The baby had eaten some meat out of a jar and now was catching huge baby Zs. We Frenched for over an hour without getting off of the couch in the living room. Then I unbuttoned the front of her shirt, a big man's shirt with the sleeves rolled up. Her bra unhooked in the front, but I couldn't do it so Maxine unsnapped it for me, grinning at me. Her nipples got hard like Hershey's Kisses. I leaned my head on her shoulder with my eyes closed and I thought about Stephanie Scotch and me moving in and out of the fluffy cloud in first grade. I even put my hand between Maxine's legs and rubbed near her thing, but I still don't know the exact count on holes down there, because she only let me do it for a minute or two. Then she clamped her legs so hard on my wrist I thought it was going to snap.

It was a good thing we didn't get off the couch, because if I had stood up Godzilla the Zipper-Buster might have actually shown. I knew Maxine Myna was not ready to meet that particular monster.

Then I had made the pretty lame mistake of breaking a lamp. We had stopped making out and were smacking a pillow from the couch back and forth between us. It was stupid, but it was flirty too, because we got to rank on each other's smacks every time we hit the pillow, and that for some reason was flirty, even if I couldn't tell you why.

But one of my shots went way wild and edged over this porcelain lamp on an end table. It had a painted picture of an old stooped Japanese man who was leaning on a long stick. He's looking into a pond where this black swan is swimming away from him with this really stuck-up look on its stupid black swan face.

Maxine got very mad.

"Now you have to wait for the Rubys to get home to explain to them that I didn't do it," she said.

"Wouldn't it be smarter for you to say you did it?" I was trying to wuss out and crawl home with my middle leg between my legs.

"No, it wouldn't."

So I had to hang out at the Rubys house until 1 AM when they came back from their party. Mr. Ruby had his tie loosened, and Mrs. Ruby had her keys out when they came through the front door, so I'll bet Mr. Ruby had had too much too drink. They were usually pretty nice—they were pretty young themselves, for grown-ups, so they were nice to their baby-sitters and told you where all the good food was and that you could sleep in their bed if you got sleepy.

But Rule # 1 of babysitting is no friends, particularly not boyfriends. Mr. Ruby frowned like his forehead was made out of Playdough when he saw me standing behind Maxine with my hands in my pockets and this please-don't-kick-my-ass look on my face.

"Why are you here, Digby?"

Mrs. Ruby kicked off her high heels and zoomed past us over to the steps. "Is the baby all right?"

I waited for Maxine to say something, but I told you that sometimes she can be a little bit of a dim bulb, so I started. "The baby's fine, Mrs. Ruby. I broke one of your lamps, and it was all my fault, and not Maxine's fault at all. She didn't even want me to come in, but I told her I had to go to the bathroom, so she let me in. I was just playing around. I didn't mean it. I'll pay for the lamp."

Mrs. Ruby came back down the steps. "What lamp?" she said. She sounded even more concerned than when she had been asking about the baby.

Maxine's brain finally switched on. "The green one by the sofa in the living room."

"OH MY GOD NOT THE CHINESE ANTIQUE! TELL ME YOU DID-N'T BREAK THE CHINESE ANTIQUE!"

I knew deep down that I was being cursed and punished for making out and reading about a carrot in a deaf girl's crack, and other wrong stuff I had been doing lately, so naturally I had broken the Tiffany lamp. It was worth about $195 and would take me until I was forty to pay off. Then Mr. Ruby called up Mr. Myna next door, and he came over in his bathrobe and chewed me out and made Maxine cry. She was some fox when she was crying.

Maxine's father made me nervous. I already said that he cried when he yelled at Jake, and then Jake would have a nervous bust-down and cry too, which was usually impossible, since Jake was the toughest guy I knew. Second, Mr. Myna was huge—tall and really pale, but his skin got really reddish when he was angry, or drinking beer, or if he stayed in the sun too long. He had forearms like Popeye that looked like giant mutant turkey legs.

Sometimes I don't know who hates me more, my ma or my father, but the competition was fierce at 2:30 that morning. My ma was just hanging up the phone as I crawled into the kitchen.

"That was Babs Ruby," my ma said. "You've got some explaining to do, mister."

As punishment I had to go to a loser party at Brenda Breschbay's house. It was a party that a bunch of the biggest loser girls in the eighth grade were having for themselves, since they never got invited to cool parties. They didn't invite any of the cool guys to their party. None of them would have gone, anyway. They only invited the middle guys and the nerds. I'm somewhere between the middle guys and the nerds.

I hemmed and hawed when Patty Pam, Pete's fat sister, finally got me on the phone. The first time I wouldn't even take the phone call, after my ma told me who it was.

"Tell her I'm out," I hissed down from the top of the stairs.

"Why, Digby? Is something the matter?" my ma called back up in her loudest voice ever.

"I'll tell you about it after you get rid of her!" Then I waited. I sat at the top of the steps like a three-year-old for my ma's voice to stop rattling on and on in the kitchen. I have listened to my ma talk on the phone for at least a million hours, so I can usually tell you exactly what she's going to say, depending on who it is, because she can't control herself when she's talking on the phone. Finally, the phone got put back on the receiver. My ma walked out of the kitchen drying her hands on a towel.

"I don't know why you're acting so strangely. Patty Pam only wanted to ask your advice on something."

"That's what you think," I said. I was in a sweat. I couldn't keep my arms by my side. They slid, because I had pits.

"Well, what do you think she wants?"

"She wants to ask me to her dumb fat-girl loser party. I don't wanna go."

"But Digby! She has such nice skin!"

It ended up with me saying I'd call her back. I wasn't going to, and I crossed my inside fingers and told God I'd have to pay him back later. It wasn't really praying if you were just asking for stuff. You were also supposed to Praise Him, but don't tell me that He didn't know when you were faking it just to get out of a jam. By the next night, I forgot completely and called Peter Kiernan up. Patty Pam answered. I tried to change my voice automatically into a gayish whining voice, but she wasn't fooled.

"Is this Digby?" she said. It sounded like she had popcorn in the pockets of her cheeks and was pursing her lips together, like she was a poodle.

"Nyaw. Hhhhm. Resssow."

"Digby, I know that this is you. Brenda Benschbay is having a party a week from Friday. Would you like to come as my date?"

How did it always happen that I was forced to answer the wrong questions asked by the wrong person at exactly the wrong time? If I said No, my ma would have a visible cow right on the kitchen table, where she was watching me from. The very mellow Peter Kiernan's house might get ugly. Every day for the rest of the year Patty Pam would look at me in the halls at school with the same busy, I'm-not-gonna-cry look.

But if I said Yes, I would be forced to spend three hours of a Friday evening (when I could be working in the lab) being squeezed and pressed against the wall by a fat babe wearing too much perfume and rouge on her cheeks, which were as big as sofa cushions, and listening to John Denver until I died of suffocation.

"Yes," I said, like the rebo that I will always be.

Patty Pam Kiernan, as my ma would say, had beautiful skin. As Peter Kiernan would say, she had a good personality. As Sister Ted would say, she was an angel. But let me tell you what I would say.

She wasn't just fat. I'm fat. I have talked about my own fat. There's nothing wrong with fat that you can talk about, fat you act like is there.

But Patty Pam had an enormous face that was at least the size of a casserole dish, and she was probably fifty pounds heavier than me. That wasn't fat. That was just plain wrong.

If she even had breasts, I wasn't particularly interested in meeting them. I would probably have to throw a body block just to stop their forward progress. I'll give her this, just so you know I'm being honest: her hair was jet-black and shiny and pretty. It looked like somebody else's hair had ended up on her scalp by mistake. She must have curled it two times a day, but she probably had a lot of time on her hands to do that.

She always had a bag of Fritos at lunch, and she didn't get milk with the rest of us. She brought a thermos of hot soup every day. After she power-slurped it, she excused herself, and with Sister Ted's blessing falling all over her like a bunch of dandruff, Patty Pam went tottering out the door and clumping down to the water fountain.

When she came back in the classroom, she was usually still wiping her lips, which were shaped like a big purplish-red bow tie. Her eyes were as black as her hair, and she wore cat-glasses somedays, but not others, so what were we supposed to be thinking? I mean, could she see without them or not?

She did a book report last year on *Cherry Ames, Student Nurse*, the stupidest book I've ever heard about in my whole life, about a nursing student who fell in love with a handsome intern, but she wouldn't let him kiss her until he broke his leg skiing. Then she felt sorry for him and kissed him. Then she felt bad that she had kissed him and wouldn't do it again. What a tease. You would think Patty Pam had done a book report on *Elizabeth Ann Seton, Student Nurse*, Sister Ted was so enchanted. After Patty Pam had stood in front of the class and read her book report aloud, which was not a bad snooze-time for everyone else, Sister Ted kept Patty Pam up there for another fifteen minutes, talking about nursing school and medical school and hospitals and medicine, and how great everything would be for everyone if they would just care more and think about themselves less.

The party was just what I expected it to be: a bunch of nervous loser girls, and a bunch of second-rank guys. Everybody was nervous, except when Mrs. Breschbay came down with the food. Then we all loosened up, as if it took an adult to be there to make us acts like kids again.

But before she showed up with the weenies-in-blankets, seven of which I hoovered deep into my love-handles while the steam was still rising off them, we played two games of Twister. The first time was with all girls and the second time was with all boys. That was no fun. The whole point of Twister was to twist around a stacked girl and then act like your wrist gave out so you could grab at her butt on the way down.

I pulled a pretty slimy move myself during one of the Twister games. Everyone who wasn't playing was just sprawling around, on the couch and on the floor, and in two armchairs, one that had three girls in it and one that had Dave Parks in it, who was the smallest guy in the eighth grade and whose feet were barely touching the floor. He had been invited by Brenda Breschbay who was handling him by not ever looking him in the eye or speaking to him, unless her mother was in the room ladling out more chow or restacking the paper cups, at which time Brenda would beeline over to him, wherever he was, and practically fall down on to her knees so that she could slip underneath his arm and make it look like they were a couple. God knows what Mrs. Breschbay thought, besides that her daughter was a borderline slut. Maybe she was also wondering how a circus midget got into her house?

The girls who were all jammed in the chair together were too nervous to sit next to a guy. Peter and I were sitting at either end of this shaggy old sofa, and in between us was Effie Whelpmin, who was from some damn place like Yugoslavia. She had done something to her boobs in her sweater, and they were like perfect triangles. Eddie Claypool came over and squeezed in between me and Effie, and started smoothing on her.

Peter had his hand up over his head, and he was flicking on and off the light. Every time he turned it off, the girls would shriek and the guys would all moan like horn dogs. Finally, one time with the light off, I couldn't stand it. I reached across in front of Eddie and grabbed a silky soft handful of Effie's tits. She screamed and the lights came back on and she turned and faced Eddie, who was grinning at her, and she slapped him across the face so hard it sounded like she broke his cheek.

"Chhow dare you!" Effie shouted.

"What?" Eddie said.

"Hue grawbbed me!"

Eddie was clueless. "I didn't grab anybody." Effie had her mouth wide open and her cheeks were red and Eddie was kind of cringing right next to her, holding his cheek in one hand and holding the other hand straight in front of him to keep her from slugging him again.

"I guess it wass a ghost!" Effie screamed next. Then Peter flicked the light again and Eddie Claypool, who wasn't there with anybody to begin with, but sneaked in with me and Peter because he was so gross girls were afraid of him, recovered. He slithered off the sofa with his legs onto the floor and walked like a crab across the floor on his hands with his pelvis tilted up in the air, and when he got in front of the armchair he slammed down one of his feet into Dave Park's nads. Everybody thought that was great.

Dave shuffled to the bathroom. Then Eddie took his place next to Effie on the sofa. Next thing I knew he had his arm around her, and she was leaning into him. He flicked his finger against my shoulder, and I looked behind Effie's head at him.

Slick, ain't I? he mouthed at me.

Next Patty Pam Kiernan tried to get a game of Truth or Dare going, with me as her victim.

"Digby, who do you have a crush on right now?"

I was not falling for that. I just grinned at her and tried to mentally blow on my eyes so they would stop burning.

"If you don't answer me, I get to dare you," Patty Pam squealed.

"Dare me instead," Peter Kiernan said to his sister.

"Okay. I dare you to go in the closet with Melissa with lights out for five minutes."

Melissa had invited Peter to the party and she was really pretty, in disguise. The cool clique hadn't discovered her, because she had only transferred into St. Tabasco at the beginning of eighth grade, which was really too late to be considered cool. She had long black eyelashes and reddish brown hair and really nice-looking arms. I call them nice-looking because they weren't muscular and they weren't fat. They were white and tight-looking. She had a silver bracelet around her left wrist like she was a princess. It had the name of a prisoner of war in Vietnam on it. She was wearing it so he wouldn't be forgotten. I talked with her about it a little bit. That was pretty cool of her.

Cissy Snodgrass was also at the party. She was the only one there who had anything to do with the cool clique, who put up with her, just like the dog clique did. She was so weird she could do anything she wanted. She was staring at me when Peter and Melissa were in the closet. We all gathered around Slim Mars, who was timing them. Cissy had brought Slim Mars but only because you had to bring somebody. She hadn't said one word to him, and he hadn't said one word to her. Her crush on him must have disappeared. He stuck to me like a grass stain on my pants, which wasn't too bad, because that way I could act like I wanted to talk to him, and ignore Patty Pam Kiernan.

"I have a truth or dare for Digby," Cissy said to Brenda.

"It's not your turn," I shouted at her. I looked at Brenda for support. Brenda looked at me and then at Cissy, because it was her party and she could be on anybody's side she wanted to.

Cissy said, "I don't care if it's not my turn."

Brenda said, "It's Slim's turn, Cissy."

"He said I could swap with him," Cissy said.

Everybody looked at Slim. He looked up and then looked at his watch. "Uh..."

"It's your turn, Slim," Brenda told him.

"Uh." Slim looked at me. There was a lot of silence as Slim realized that there was nothing embarassing he could stand to ask me without being embarassed himself.

Then the party seemed to pick back up, and there was cake, and we watched home movies of when Brenda Breschbay was a baby and the candles flickered like little strips of clear plastic. But I didn't really have too much fun.

There was a little bit of action when we were getting ready to leave. Effie Whelpmin was at the party with Leo Oliosy, and we thought they were making out at one point because nobody could find them. But they were both in the bathroom taking turns throwing up.

Patty Pam and Peter and Melissa and I walked home afterward. The moon had risen up into the middle of the sky. It was still orange like it was when it had just come out, and it made the night feel warm. Patty Pam was trying to hold my hand, and every time she grabbed it, I acted like she was hurting me and ran ahead a few steps, yelling. It was not the least gay reaction I could have had. Peter and Melissa were walking behind us. He had his arm around her.

We cut through town and wasted some time twisting the levers on all the parking meters just to hear them rattle. Then Peter and I had a contest. We tried to spit in the air and then catch it back into our mouths again, which was a smart move on my part, because it grossed Patty Pam out and she stopped trying to hold my hand, but it was a stupid move on the part of Peter for exactly the same reason, because Melissa got grossed out and wouldn't walk with him any more. So he and I walked together, behind the girls.

We passed by Willard's Flower Shop. I pressed my face against the glass window and held my hand on my forehead to shade the glare from the streetlamps, but I couldn't see jack. Peter and I took turns trying to jump and hit the fringe on the green-striped awning in front of the shop, and the girls sat down on the curb to wait for us. Peter and I did that for a while, and then we all just went home.

Graduation Dance

On the Saturday before the eighth grade graduation dance, I also got invited to a cool party. I thought it was going to be another shot with Maxine, but it turned out to be a waste of time.

First I should tell you about this huge rumor that the guys in the eighth grade had started about getting on base with girls. Fitz Patrick said that his older brother had a book that listed all the bases, not just first, second, third, and home base, which everybody knew about, if they weren't babies. In this book Fitz was talking about there were 150 bases. I don't know all of them, but Fitz Patrick says that for 121st base, you cut off a girl's tit and fried it in a frying pan, which was totally gross, but sort of hilarious, if you weren't a girl.

I was in the kitchen at one point at the cool party, and saw a tiny frying pan hanging on a nail above the stove. It said "Hershey PA" on it. At the cool party, there were no little silly gay games, like there had been at Brenda Breschbay's disastrous loser-girl party a couple of weeks earlier. At cool parties, you were either just broken-up with somebody, in which case you sat out in the living room and cursed, or maybe snuck out onto the carport to smoke a cigarette, or you were making out. I knew people were making out in a little bedroom right off the kitchen, so I stood by the door. I could hear little giggles and breathing inside. I shoved open the door, flicked on the light, and yelled, "Anybody get to 121st yet?"

When I burst through the bedroom door, there were five couples sprawled around the room. Two couples were on the floor, and two couples were squeezed onto the bed, and there was another couple jammed into the bottom of the closet on top of all these shoes and shoe trees. I could hear them bumping around in there. The closet door was making wheely noises. I got some pretty big yuks with the frying pan, so at first I was pumped and thought I was a stud, the way you do sometimes at first if you get off a good line, but before you realize the joke's on you. Even if I wasn't in there sucking face, I was at least cool enough to *interrupt* the ones who were sucking face, which usually would be the worst thing a person could do, and get a laugh at the same time.

Then I saw this hand with a black wingtip shoe in it come out of the closet. Connected to it was Maxine Myna. She was wearing white painter overalls, except one of the overall straps was down off her shoulder, so her bra was showing. Connected to Maxine Myna was this guy named Tony who got kicked out of our school last year for smoking pot. Now he goes to public school and wears pooka beads and his eyes are always red.

So that was that.

I slunk out like a skunk without his stink and waited around like a pathetic loser for Maxine to crawl out of the back room with Mr. Pooka so I could give her a piece of my mind.

When Maxine did come out of the room, she was not with Tony.

"Where is *he*?" I asked, like I wasn't even going to say his name.

She gave me this dopey wide-eyed look like she hadn't seen me two minutes before when she had been sucking face. "Are you talking about Tony?"

"Who do ya think I'm talking about?" I felt like crying.

"Lynn Michaels grabbed him. I'm not going out with him." Now Maxine was pissed at him too. She also smelled like beer. Her belt buckle looked like it was loose, and I could see one black hair in her belly button. Suddenly, I was back in love with her, more than ever before.

Fitz walked by me and said, "Hey, Maxine, you wanna get back together?"

"Sure," Maxine said. He put his arm around her waist and they walked back to the bedroom. I sat on the counter in the kitchen flipping the little frying pan over in my hand for a while. Then I plowed through a box of Scooter Pies and was out of there.

I don't worry about the daydream anymore. I don't think I'd like to be back in third grade. I might be remembering it wrong altogether, because my ma told me the night of the graduation dance, at dinner, that back then I used to cry on Sunday nights, because it meant I had to go to school the next day.

"I did not."

"You did so. Everyone would take their bath, and then we'd watch *Animal Kingdom*. When it was over, it was time for bed, and you would sob."

"Don't lie!"

"Don't call your mother a liar," my father said.

"*You* call her a liar," Maud said to him. Then my father just glared around the room at everybody.

"Yes you did cry, Digby. I could sit and watch your face as you realized it was time to sleep, and then wake up, and then go to school. You hated the third grade," my ma said.

"What are you talking about? I loved the third grade. I used to dream about it."

"No, you liked the fourth grade. You hated third grade. I had to stop putting notes in your lunchbox at lunch because you'd cry at recess. The monitor would call me up to chew me out for making you homesick."

So maybe I got it wrong. I thought about it as I put on my blue velour shirt to wear to the graduation dance. I took a long bath and washed my nads about fifty times. I had never been to a dance before, and you never know. Maybe everybody would be having sex. I wanted to be ready.

Maud still tries to make me feel bad for fooling around with her friend.

"I can't believe you tried to attack Margaret," Maud said to me. I was waiting for my hair to dry.

"What are you talking about? Who told you that?"

"She did."

"She's crazy. I didn't try to attack anyone."

"She says you did. Don't try to deny that you fooled around with her."

I did want to deny that I had fooled around with her. Swapping spit is not something you really want to go into in detail with your sister. But I was stuck. I had to explain the truth.

"We messed around a little. But she wanted to!"

"You're gross. Leave my friends alone."

"At least I don't make out with a weasel-face," I told her. I was referring to Rafe, but that was a stupid way to put it, since Maud was in love with him and so she wouldn't think he looked like a weasel. Plus she doesn't know squat about animals. I doubt if she's ever even seen a weasel.

❀ ❀ ❀

At the eighth grade graduation dance, things were tense for a while, just because most of us had never danced before, and nobody had ever danced in front of our parents. A lot of them were there, since Sister Ted had made us invite them all. My father didn't come. He stayed at home with Molly. But my ma did. She left me alone most of the time, but I knew she was watching me. We had punch in plastic punchbowls and cookies, and they played a lot of Elton John. More and more kids were starting in dancing as time went on.

When I first walked in, Sister Ted waved at me and I waved back. Then I noticed she had sneakers on. I must have been staring, because she asked me what was wrong.

"You're wearing sneakers. I never saw you wearing sneakers before."

"They're not sneakers," Sister Ted huffed. "They're canvas deck shoes." She went off and danced with Bartos Cuscousmontrous. Neither of them were very good dancers. They looked like they were stepping up and down on a stepladder.

I was staying out of it. The only time I had ever danced was with Molly in our basement during the intro music to *Happy Days*, where Molly stood on the front of my feet and I duck-walked around with her arms around my neck. I was chatting with a bunch of girls, though, cool ones and nerds, and Slim Mars was hanging around behind me just about on my heel, so I wasn't feeling lonely.

Then, all of a sudden, it was as if I had been changed completely. I heard a new song start, and a fiddle start scratching, and everybody in the church hall was clapping their hands, and I felt my feet start tapping.

> *Well life on a farm is kinda laid back,*
> *Ain't much an old country boy like me can hack.*
> *It's early to rise, early in the sack:*
> *Thank God I'm a country boy.*

I could see my ma smiling at me from the other end of the hall. I walked over to her, and poked her arm through my arm, and started swinging her around and around me as fast as I could. Don't get me wrong. I wasn't trying to fake like I was a hick who lived on a farm and had a southern accent. I just couldn't resist it. My whole body was twitching to the music. It made me want to run and jump and sing and swing, like I was a little kid who had just been let go outside after spending the whole morning at his great grandmother's house playing jacks on a dusty carpet in the living room.

> *Well, my fiddle was my daddy's till the day he died,*
> *and he took me by the hand and held me close to his side.*
> *He said: "Live a good life and play my fiddle with pride,*
> *and thank God you're a country boy."*

I looked at my ma, and she was smiling at me. I looked and saw Slim Mars standing at the edge of the dance floor, and he was looking at me and smiling and stomping his foot up and down, and slapping his hand against his thigh. I felt somebody brush by my shoulder, and it was Maxine Myna dancing with her dad, who had his hand over her head holding her hand, and he was twirling her like she was on a rubber band that he had wound up too tight.

> *Well, I got me a fine wife, I got me an old fiddle.*
> *When the sun's comin' up I got cakes on the griddle;*
> *And life ain't nothin' but a funny, funny riddle:*
> *Thank God I'm a country boy.*

It could have been that the song mentioned pancakes, which always did me in, since I could eat them until the cows came home, but I don't think so. I was happy. The world was pretty nice, and I couldn't resist singing along.

I got a letter from Peter right after he moved to Michigan somewhere. His parents had enrolled him in a school without walls. It was for bright kids who were motivated by themselves and didn't need discipline. The whole thing sounded super hippie to me, and, in fact, Peter used the word "groovy" about five times in the letter.

In the very first sentence Peter said he missed me, but that Michigan was "groovy." Then he asked why I hadn't written him? There was also a hilarious description of some girls in his new neighborhood. About this one girl, Melissa, Peter wrote "She's really, really good-looking and groovy, but big." It was just like him to be really into something, and also very honest about it at the same time.

The letter made me sad. Then he wrote for me to go by his old house and check to make sure their car was still there.

Peter also asked in a P.S. if I would give or sell him my Frank Howard poster. Peter knew it was one of my prize possessions, so I guess he was getting greedy, being in a completely new state. He probably just wanted some stuff around that reminded him of his old home. But he's still not going to get it.

I guess that someday I'll be remembering all of this again. That's probably how life goes—everything again and again. By then I hope I'm somebody else, somebody who can look back at this whole eighth-grade mess and laugh his ass off.

Who knows who will be laughing then? Will I be a serious scientist who's pretty smart, but who doesn't have time for laughs and crazy stuff, because he has to keep his brain pretty much swept clean for all the important, complicated stuff he'll be doing, typing blood like old Richard Drew, or creating electricity like Steinmetz, who was partially a dwarf.

Maybe I'll be a politician in a car nineteen hours a day going to meet my voters. Swinging my long Democrat legs out of my car, I'll walk up a short brick path to tell some old lady about how things are in congress and how she better stick with me since I'm the only politician who's ever bothered to come through her door and shake her hand.

Maybe I'll work for the government, and sigh a lot when I get home when I don't think anybody is listening, like my father. I won't want to talk about what I do at work. I'll just tell anybody who asks, It's so boring I'd fall asleep on my feet if I started telling you about it. That is actually one of my father's better lines.

Maybe I'll have four kids like he and my ma have, although I hope I get a girlfriend first. Maybe I'll be famous, which I sometimes think about being, even though I wouldn't have the first idea how to become famous.

I'd just want to be born famous. Famous like a king or a Kennedy, some-body who didn't have to do squat to make the news, who had so much money it would make you sick.

People would see me coming and think to themselves, That Digby Shaw, everybody knows him, everybody wants to hear what he thinks about things. What made him so lucky?

Even thinking about getting older, and having to do a ton more things that I've never done before, gives me this strange stomachy feeling. It's like I'm already supposed to be busy. Hopefully, things will just come along in my life a couple at a time, so I can handle them. Maybe I'll just sneak through, be an adult and have a job and have a girlfriend, and not have to worry too much about it. But first the girlfriend.

To me the past looks like my old scrapbook. It's stupid and awkward and big, and I just stuck things into it because I didn't want to take the time to put a little scotch tape on them. It looks dumb, the past, but if you crack it open a little bit you can find some pretty interesting stuff, if somebody comes along with you to point out the sights.

The present is like this long morning where you're watching the clock and you're hungry already but lunch is not coming fast enough. You just have to keep on doing whatever you're doing and hope ol' 12 o'clock comes along, and that maybe there's an extra milk at lunch, or something cool is going on at recess like a game of maul ball, where you can get a good stick in on someone and spear them and dump them on their head.

The future doesn't look like anything. Maybe it looks like a book I haven't read, and may not like, but will probably read anyway sometime just for the hey of it.

Chris Scrivens

SEAN ENRIGHT was born in Washington, DC and grew up in Maryland, where he lives with his wife and children. His poems have appeared in numerous literary magazines, including Threepenny Review, The Kenyon Review, Sewanee Review, and The Southern Poetry Review. **Goof and Other Stories** is his first book with Creative Arts.